A Proper Place

Also by Joan Lingard

The Twelfth Day of July
Across the Barricades
Into Exile

The Clearance
Frying as Usual

A Proper Place

JOAN LINGARD

THOMAS NELSON INC., PUBLISHERS
Nashville   New York

Copyright © 1975 by Joan Lingard

First U.S. edition

All rights reserved under International and Pan-American Conventions.

Published by Thomas Nelson, Inc., Publishers, Nashville, Tennessee.
Manufactured in the United States of America.

TO THE MEMORY
OF
HONOR ARUNDEL
who first encouraged me to
start writing about Sadie and Kevin

Library of Congress Cataloging in Publication Data
Lingard, Joan.
  A proper place.
  SUMMARY: A Protestant girl and a Catholic boy from Northern Ireland
cope with family members, the baptism of their child, and a move from the
Liverpool slums to a Cheshire farm.
  [1. Family life—Fiction] I. Title.
PZ7.L6626Pr   [Fic]   75–6591
ISBN 0–8407–6425–1

Chapter One

"ME MA's coming to visit us," said Sadie McCoy the moment her husband Kevin opened the door and set foot in the kitchen. All day she had been waiting for him, wondering how she was going to get round to telling him, and now it had popped out, just as quickly as that, without her even having had to try to lead up to it.

"*What?*"

Kevin's khaki satchel dropped to the floor like a stone. Sadie busied herself picking it up, opening it, taking out the vacuum flask and sandwich box. She did not look near his face.

"You didn't finish your sandwiches. That's not like you."

"Sadie, you're having me on! About your mother ..."

"No, I'm not." She looked up at him then. "She's coming. Saturday. I had the letter this morning." She took it from her apron pocket; it was crumpled for it had been read many times.

"But Sadie—!"

"Now don't you start! I didn't ask her. She's just coming."

"But we have no place for her," said Kevin, knowing of course that had nothing to do with it.

"She can sleep on the settee." Sadie nodded at the sagging piece of furniture in the corner. The room served as living room as well as kitchen. "She won't stay long. A night on that ould thing and her back'll be bothering her something awful." Sadie grinned, in spite of herself, for she could usually find a funny side to most things.

At the moment Kevin could see nothing amusing about the prospect at all. He was dead tired, he had worked all day on a building site which had been turned into a sea of wet mud by steady driving rain, and now what he wanted was to have a good wash, sit down and eat his tea and not have to think about his mother-in-law. He had never even set eyes on her, and was content that it should stay that way. From the sound of her, that is, from the way her daughter talked of her, he thought it highly unlikely that he would be able to put up with her at all, let alone like her. She was an Orangewoman, with a mural of King Billy on the gable end of her house and a picture of the Queen and the Duke of Edinburgh above her mantelpiece, whilst he, Kevin was a Catholic. He had taken her Protestant daughter out of Ireland, brought her to England and married her, so how could she ever begin to like him either? It would be a hopeless case from the start. He groaned as he eased off his boots.

"I don't much fancy her coming myself, you know," said Sadie, "but what can I do?" In fact, underneath, she was quite excited by the idea of her mother coming, even though they always ended up arguing.

"Send her a telegram. Tell her we've all got cholera. What's she wanting to come for anyway? She's not bothered before."

"She wants to see her grandson of course. What else? I'm sure it's not to see me. Or you."

As if on cue, the grandson began to cry in the next room. He was two months old and strong for his age, with a power-ful set of lungs. He took after his mother in that respect, said Kevin. Sadie went to fetch him. The noise ceased like a tap being turned off as soon as she lifted him.

"Isn't he the one?" she said, shaking her head, as she brought him through to the kitchen. "The size of him, and getting his own way!"

"You'll not need to spoil him now, Sadie. I'm not wanting a namby-pamby for a son."

6

"Fat chance he'll get to be a namby-pamby round here! By the time he grows up in this place he'll be ready to join the guerillas."

They were living in Liverpool. After crossing over on the boat from Belfast there had been no money to go any further so they had found a room and Kevin a job. They had meant to stay only a month or two and then move on. That was well over a year ago.

Before the baby was born they had searched and searched and finally found these two rooms on the ground floor of a three-storeyed terraced house. The area had once been good, in the days when Liverpool herself was rich and grand, when the shipping trade flourished and money flowed freely. Now the population of the city had declined, and money with it, and most of those who had any had taken it and gone to live in the Wirral, the peninsula between the Dee and Mersey rivers, leaving the centre for those who were not so well off and for some young professional people who were "doing up" old houses. They had one such couple in their street who were out at work all day and came and went in a red sports car which the kids scratched and clambered over. They had painted their door purple, and they had been burgled three times.

Their terrace was early Victorian. Apart from the house with the purple door, paint was peeling, stone work going scabby, window frames decaying, roofs leaking, gutter pipes overflowing. It was a long time since a landlord had done any repairs. Some houses were empty and had broken windows, others were boarded up.

Several families lived in Sadie and Kevin's house. The building buzzed with noise all day long, and often half the night as well: kids shouting and crying, feet clattering, televisions blaring. You got used to it after a bit, more or less. Not that Sadie and Kevin intended to stay. This was only temporary, until they could get something better, and they were certainly not going to bring up Brendan here. Water ran down the walls in wet weather, the wallpaper looked as if it had measles where it was not hanging loose, and there was no shortage of mice on the scrounge. Rats too, said some. No place for a baby, said Sadie daily. Kevin said nothing but his face tightened, and then Sadie, not liking to see him troubled, would smile and say, "Ach well, one of these days ..."

"Will you hold the wee fellow a minute?" Sadie put Brendan into his father's arms. "I want to run along to the shop."

Kevin held the baby clumsily, letting the small head dangle backwards. Sadie rearranged it so that it was supported against Kevin's arm.

"You're a right eejit when it comes to holding babies. You'd think he was stuffed with straw the way you hold him."

"Away ye go, wumman, and leave us men till ourselves!"

Sadie stuck out her tongue at him and lifted her purse from the sideboard. For once she knew where it was! Kevin said she should have it tied around her neck on a piece of string. She ran along the pavement dodging children, old tyres, battered bicycles, old prams, tin cans. At the end of the street she paused to look downwards, towards the city. They had a marvellous view from here, could see the river and the outlines of the big buildings downtown. It was the same nearly everywhere you went in Liverpool: you turned a corner and there it all was, spread out below. It was hazy now and pinpricks of light were springing up like stars. Sadie loved this time of day, lights coming on, the promise of evening ahead. The days were shortening: summer had gone. But she liked autumn too, with its marvellous glowing colours and crisp sparkling air. One good thing their street did have was trees; they lined the pavement on either side. The trees in Liverpool had been a surprise to her: you could walk for miles beneath trees in the city, even through many of the streets of small red-bricked terraced houses.

She crossed the street to the shop on the opposite corner. It was busy. People always seemed to remember they'd run out of something at this time of day, and then of course there were the men coming home from their work buying cigarettes, and girls going out for the evening buying a pair of tights. It was the kind of little shop that Sadie had been used to at home in Belfast: it sold everything from potatoes, bread and milk

to tights and firelighters. It opened early, closed late. Mrs
Hignett, who owned it, bustled up and down behind the laden
counter. The lights were on, people were talking to one another whilst they waited.

"Hello there, Sadie."

She knew most people. She settled in for a chat with Mrs
Paradise who lived in their house. She was West Indian and
had come over five years ago with her husband and five
children. Two more had been born since their arrival. Her
eldest, Gabriel, who was sixteen, was a constant source of
worry to her. He was in trouble again.

"I just don't know what to do with that boy! The police
come this morning. Didn't you see them? He's been smashing
telephone boxes and writing slogans on people's walls. I'll
slogan him when I catch him!" Mrs Paradise rolled her black
eyes. "And his dad can't do nothing with him."

Sadie sympathised, thinking that this could never happen
to Brendan. How could that small sweet child ever turn into
a wild hooligan that not even his father could do a thing
with? Kevin would see to it that he did not, and so would
she. But inside herself she knew you could never be sure of
a thing like that.

"I tell you, Sadie, kids are nothing but a sorrow."

"Ah come on now, Mrs Paradise, you don't mean that at
all. Sure isn't your Maria one of the nicest girls you could
ever lay eyes on?'

Ah well maybe so, Mrs Paradise admitted, for Maria, a year
younger than Gabriel, was good and kind and thoughtful,
and had a happy nature too. She was forever to be heard singing and laughing in the house. In fact, her mother did not
know what she would do without her. Maria spent a lot of
time with Sadie and the baby and she fed him if Sadie wanted
to go out. When Sadie brought him home from hospital feeling
as if she had ten thumbs Maria had come to the rescue. She
could bath babies blindfold, change them, comfort them,
and no matter how much they screamed she never fussed.
Sadie had never had anything to do with babies before she
had Brendan and the sight of the small red-faced bundle

dependent on her for his every need had terrified her.

It was Mrs Paradise's turn now to be served. Sadie glanced round as the door jangled open again and saw her special friend Kitty coming in. Kitty also lived in their house, with her husband Bill and baby son David.

Kitty joined Sadie, put her basket between her feet.

"What a day it's been!" she said, shaking out her long dark hair. "That kid's nearly driven me round the bend. Have you heard him? The whole street must have done. I wish his tooth would come through and be done with it."

Sadie and Kitty walked the streets and parks of Liverpool together pushing their prams. Bill and Kevin were friendly too and went to football matches on Saturday afternoons. And then, in the evening, on Saturdays, they would gather, drink beer, have some food, talk and play records. Sadie looked forward to Saturday nights.

"How did Kevin take the news about your mother?" asked Kitty.

Sadie made a face. "You couldn't say he was off his head with delight exactly."

'Well then, Sadie, what are you wanting?" said Mrs Hignett. "You're next."

"Packet of fish fingers."

Coming out of the shop Sadie met Maria Paradise who was on her way home from school.

"You're late home the night."

"Music club."

Maria liked to sing and also play the guitar. She was learning at school, but had no guitar of her own and little likelihood of getting one. She worked in a shop on Saturdays and had tried saving but her mother was constantly in need of money for Mr Paradise was out of work more than he was in.

Sadie and Maria stood on the doorstep of the house for a few minutes before going inside. Light was going fast from the street now. From high up in the house they could hear the wail of the youngest Paradise, Crystal.

"I'd better go." Maria heaved up the books under her arm. She climbed the stairs. Sadie went into their flat which was on the ground floor, to the right of the door. To the left lived an aged widow, Mrs Francie, who was seldom seen. Every now and then Sadie imagined the worst; she would listen outside her door for a while trying to hear sounds within, and then, convinced that the old soul must be lying dead or unconscious, she would knock and call out, "Are you there, Mrs Francie?" After a bit Mrs Francie would open the door and just about eat the head off her for getting her out of bed and after that Sadie would vow never again, she could stew for all she cared!

Kevin was talking to Brendan in a soft cooing voice.

"He's going to be a bright lad," said Kevin. "You can tell already by the look in his eye."

"Like his da!"

Sadie lit the gas and put the frying pan on the ring. She glanced over at Kevin and the baby and felt warm right down to the middle of her.

"We'll just have to make the best of it, Kev. My mother coming, I mean."

"Aye."

"I'll buy her a bottle of port to sweeten her up. She likes a drop. Not that she'd admit it of course." Sadie grinned. "She keeps a bottle locked in the cupboard in the front parlour."

"I don't know if we've enough money for that, Sadie."

"Surely you wouldn't deny my mother a wee drop of port—"

"I'm not wanting to deny her anything. But you seem to forget we've the telly to pay for on Friday and there's the next payment on the pram. Money's a terrible worry."

"You don't have to tell *me* that."

"But Sadie, you're the one that spends more than we've said. You get carried away—"

Sadie broke in. "Carried away is it? Just look at me in this beautiful dream kitchen with all the latest gadgets!"

"All right, Sadie, there's no call to talk like that. I don't like it much either. But we have to be careful."

"If we have to be that careful we might as well be ten feet

under." Sadie dropped the fish fingers into the pan. "So you'd deny me mother a bottle of port would you, Kevin McCoy? And do we not send *your* mother three pounds every week of our lives? If we didn't have to do that we might not be as poor as we are."

"I can't help that," said Kevin abruptly.

"You could if you wanted to."

"She needs the money."

"So do I."

There was silence for a moment except for the spitting of the fat in the pan. Sadie glanced at him and saw that he would not reply. She hated it when he closed up tight, it made her worse and want to needle him, to sting him into saying more.

"Why should your wife and child suffer for the sake of your mother? Which comes first do you reckon?"

"You do, you know that."

"But three pounds is a lot of money every week—"

Kevin got up and went through to the bedroom. He laid the baby in the cot, took off his jacket and sat down on the bed. Sadie followed him as far as the doorway where she stood watching him, the fish slice in her hand.

"Gerald's working now, isn't he?" she said.

"Gerald's not much use to anyone. She can't rely on him. You know I had to promise the money so that I could leave. You agreed."

"What else could I do? I wanted you to come with me."

Kevin's father had been killed by a bomb in a pub, leaving his mother a widow with nine children to bring up. It was to Kevin, the eldest son, that she had turned for help. She had wanted him to stay with her but had not wanted his Protestant wife with him.

Kevin lay back on the bed with his hands behind his head. He stared at the ceiling. He looked very weary. Sadie crumpled suddenly at the sight of him. She ran to the bed and knelt beside him.

"Are you for whacking me with that thing, then?" He eyed the fish slice.

She laughed, laying it aside. "I'm sorry, Kev, I didn't mean it. I know you've got to help your mother. I don't really grudge it, it's just that sometimes—" She sighed, and nestled her head against his shoulder.

"And I'm sorry, too, Sadie, that I've no more money to give you."

"You do your best, love, I know that. And when Brendan's bigger I'll be able to get a job again, part-time at least. I'll put him in a nursery when he's a year old."

"I don't want you to have to do that." He stroked her silky fair hair.

"Ach, we'll be all right, I know we will. Sure, haven't we come through all sorts of things?"

Kevin sniffed. "There's something burning."

"Glory be!" cried Sadie, leaping to her feet. "It's me fish fingers!"

Chapter Two

THE BELFAST boat was coming in as Sadie reached the Pier Head, but it would be a little while before it docked and the passengers disembarked and came through the sheds, so she had time to spare. She had come out early so that she would, for she loved it here, down the river. It was seldom that she came downtown, because of Brendan.

She walked along the pier, the hood of her anorak pulled up. It was a chilly, damp morning. Sea gulls were wheeling and crying, pigeons hopping about hopefully. A ship's siren bellowed out, deep and loud. Sadie leant on the rail and looked across the Mersey at the gantries on the far shore marking the shipyards at Birkenhead. That was a familiar-looking sight: it reminded her of Belfast. She had a lump in her throat. That wouldn't do at all! She swallowed, moved on. No point in getting all sentimental. Still, she did like the look of the gantries and the ships and the river, and the smell of it too. The smells in particular took her back to the night in Belfast when she had run off with Kevin. She had waited for him in the sheds, trembling and excited, but with no doubts about going. And she still had no doubts that she had done the right thing.

The Belfast boat had gone into a special dock where the public were not allowed, unless travelling. Security was tight, and needed to be. She would meet her mother in the waiting room of the Belfast Steamship Company: that was as far as she was allowed to go. She imagined her mother waiting below in the warmth of the saloon—she would not be lining the deck rail—keeping a firm grip of her luggage in case anyone would run off with it.

Sadie continued along the pier. She pushed off her hood, shook her hair free into the wind. She passed the small ferry boats that made the trip to and from Wallasey. Then there was a bigger boat that plied between Liverpool and the Isle of Man. They must go over to the island some time; one of these days when they had a bit of money to spare. She stopped to take a closer look at the small tug boats. She wouldn't mind a trip up river in one of those. She wouldn't mind a trip anywhere. She had always fancied travelling, used to see herself boarding liners, setting sail, for San Francisco and the Orient. You couldn't go far from Liverpool now, only Belfast and the Isle of Man. Once you could travel the world over from here, but now all the big liners had moved down to Southampton. Its heyday was over, Mrs Hignett was always saying, but still, Sadie liked the old place, it had a few things in its favour. Not their street of course, not that.

She turned back. The city was on her left now. They were cleaning up some of the old buildings, removing the soot that had collected over the years. They looked very fine, especially the three big ones along the waterfront, the Harbour Board, Cunard and Liver Buildings. Yes, the city looked all right from down here.

A passing seaman turned and whistled at Sadie. Little did he know she was a married woman and a mother! She knew she didn't look it, in her old jeans and anorak and her hair tied back with a piece of green ribbon. She did not feel it much either, except when Brendan screamed half the night and she got no sleep.

She went to the waiting room. A number of people sat or stood about. She leant against the wall watching the door through which the passengers would come.

A few minutes later they began to trickle through. For a

moment Sadie did not recognise her mother for she had half expected to see her in her wrap-around overall and rollers, as she usually was at home. Sadie realised that she had not often been outside with her mother, not since she was small. In her mind her mother belonged in the kitchen frying ham and eggs, doing the ironing and gossiping to Mrs Mullet who had just dropped in to borrow a couple of eggs or whatever she could lay hands on. Today Mrs Jackson wore a new bright purple coat trimmed with fur round the collar, and a purple felt hat to match.

Sadie dodged through the crowd to her. "Hello, Ma."

"Sadie! I never thought you'd be here on time."

"Give us your case then." Sadie seized her mother's suitcase and planted a kiss on her cheek, knocking the purple hat askew. The hair beneath had been newly permed and set in neat, tight ridges.

Mrs Jackson straightened her hat and said, "Well Sadie, how are you? You've not changed much anyway." But she was pleased enough to see her, Sadie could tell that. "What are you wearing that ould anorak for? You had it at school, for dear sake."

"I like it."

Mrs Jackson shook her head.

"Come on then, Ma, let's get out of here. It's only a few steps to the bus stop."

"Thank goodness for that." Mrs Jackson grasped her arm. "My feet are nearly killing me. I bought these new shoes just the other day there and they're not broken in yet."

"You can put your slippers on when we get in. Did you have a good crossing?"

"Oh, it was desperate. I never slept a wink all night. I thought I was going to get thrown out of me bunk the way it was bucking and rearing. It was a mercy I wasn't as sick as a dog."

Sadie and Kevin had listened to the weather forecast the night before and there had been no mention of a gale. Sadie did not say so.

"You'll feel better once you've had a cup of tea."

They reached the bus stop. Sadie put the case between her feet. Mrs Jackson asked after the baby, but not Kevin.

"I don't know why you had to call the wee fellow Brendan," said Mrs Jackson with a sniff. A sniff was part of her, like a nervous tic; Sadie was used to it, but now she wondered uneasily how Kevin would accept it.

"Why not?" said Sadie, knowing full well why her mother didn't like it. It was a name that Catholics favoured.

"I could think of others I'd like better."

"Like Billy," said Sadie and giggled suddenly. It was a relief to giggle. "Good old King Billy! I could tell him about the Battle of the Boyne and teach him to sing *The Sash*."

"Now don't you start that or I'll be away home on the next boat."

"I'm sorry, Ma. I was just making a joke. Here's our bus coming."

They were quiet on the bus, each of them thinking of the arrival.

"Lots of blacks about," said Mrs Jackson, glancing round the bus.

"Shush, Ma," said Sadie fiercely.

"What's up now?"

"People'll hear you."

"I was only passing a remark. There's nothing wrong with passing a remark is there?"

"Depends what the remark is."

"We don't have as many of them in Belfast."

"Who'd want to go there?"

The bus reached their stop. They got off and Mrs Jackson looked up the street, in horror.

"You're not living here are you, Sadie? It's a slum."

"It's all we can afford. But it's only temporary. Kevin's put our name down for a council house. We'd have put it down earlier but we didn't think we'd be staying."

Mrs Jackson moved her neck from side to side above the fur collar of her purple coat, denoting disbelief, dislike and total disapproval. Sadie knew how to interpret every twitch of her mother's. Words were frequently unnecessary.

"Come on," she said irritably, leading the way.

Mrs Jackson missed nothing; every piece of litter, filth and sign of poverty were noted by her darting eyes.

"You weren't brought up in the likes of this, Sadie. Our street was the cleanest in the whole of Belfast."

"I've been waiting for you to say that. Why can't you give me a surprise sometime?" They had arrived at the house. "This is it, Ma. Step inside. Next best thing to Buckingham Palace! Princess Anne, eat your heart out!"

Mrs Jackson sniffed, with indignation, and also to savour the smells of the hallway which were many and various.

Kevin was standing in the middle of the kitchen with his hands dangling loosely by his sides. He looked as if he did not know what to do with them, his feet, or himself. There was a smell of thick stewed tea hanging in the air.

Sadie introduced them. Kevin moved forward a step to shake hands, then retreated putting his hand behind his back when it became obvious that his mother-in-law was determined to continue clasping hers firmly together in front of her stomach. She nodded the purple hat at him, said primly, "Pleased to meet you," then turned back to Sadie to demand, "Where's the wee one then?"

Sadie fetched Brendan who had just fallen into a sound sleep and was not much inclined to wake for the entertainment of his grandmother. Sadie gave him to her mother. He screwed up his face, turned a shade of puce from the soft fold of his neck right up to the bald crown of his head, and began to roar. He was furious. He lashed out blindly with his small fists. He roared and roared and would not stop.

Sadie took him back. "He's tired."

Her mother sniffed, rearranged her hat.

"I've made a pot of tea," said Kevin, who had been doing a half dance round the back of them.

Sadie poured the tea with one hand, keeping Brendan on her other arm. He struggled and screamed. She carried him back to the bedroom.

"Now go to sleep," she said as she laid him in his cot, "and show your granny what a good boy you are."

But he did not fancy being laid down either, not now. Sadie shut the door on his screams.

"He's usually very good," she said.

Her mother did not look as if she believed her. She sat on the edge of a chair, still wearing her coat and hat, holding her cup on her lap. The liquid in it was black as pitch.

"Are you hungry?" asked Sadie. "I'll cook you some ham and eggs."

Kevin cleared his throat. "I think I'll be going on out now, Sadie, if that's all right with you. I promised Bill I'd give him a hand with his motor bike. See you later, Mrs Jackson."

He left quickly. As soon as he had gone Mrs Jackson put aside the cup and saucer, unbuttoned her coat and took off her shoes. Sadie laid rashers of Irish gammon in the pan feeling as if she had those ten thumbs back again. In the other room Brendan was still yelling his head off but she thought she could detect signs that he might be flagging.

"He's got a good set of lungs on him at any rate," said her mother. "You were the very same when you were a baby. Never gave me a minute's peace."

The bacon was done too crisp for her mother's liking and Sadie broke one of her eggs when she was putting it on the plate, but Mrs Jackson was very hungry and polished off the lot, along with three slices of bread and four cups of freshly made tea.

"I feel a mite better now," she declared, sitting back. She had shed her coat before breakfast but not her hat. When she got up from the table she took the pin out and laid the hat aside, thus showing that she intended to remain for a while. She primped up the back of her hair with her hand.

"How long are you staying for, Ma?"

"You're quick to ask. Here's your hat, what's the hurry, eh?"

"I was just wondering. You're welcome to stay as long as you like, you know that." Sadie began to clear the table.

"I don't think your da could spare me more than a week."

"How is Da?"

"Doing rightly. Well, as far as anyone is in the North of

Ireland under the circumstances. He was asking after you and all that. Wishing you'd come back to see us a bit more often." Mrs Jackson sat down in the armchair again. "Are you needing a hand?"

"No, no, just you rest yourself."

"I'm needing a rest, I must admit. I'm fair done in. Where's my room, Sadie?"

"Well ..." Sadie's voice trailed off. "We only have the two rooms, ma."

"You mean—?" Mrs Jackson's eyes circled the kitchen.

"I'm afraid you'll need to sleep on the settee. I hope you don't mind."

"I can't stomach sleeping in the same room where food's been cooked." Mrs Jackson folded her arms across the chest. "It's not good for anybody that. What would your da say if he knew?"

Sadie turned on the tap angrily. She wished her mother had never come. She wished she would put her purple coat and hat back on and walk out of the room before Kevin came back. She tossed a cup into the basin catching the handle on the tap and knocking it off.

"Drat!"

"You should take your time," said her mother. "You always were terrible slapdash."

"And you always were a terrible nark," said Sadie loudly and clearly.

"What?" Mrs Jackson laid her hand against her throat. "What's that you said to me, Sadie Jackson?"

"You heard." Sadie dried her hands and turned to face her mother. "And my name's McCoy now whether you like it or not."

"You know I don't like it."

"Then what did you come for?"

Mrs Jackson's fingers trembled over her neck. "I wanted to see you. And the baby. I don't know what your da would say if he were here—"

"Well he's not. And if you're going to sit there and find fault with every single thing I do then you'd better take yourself back on the next boat. This is my house, Ma, and Kevin's."

Mrs Jackson put her hands over her face now. "Dear God, what a daughter you've been to me ... always in trouble ... never in the house ... out roaming the streets worrying the life out of me."

"That's all ages ago," said Sadie impatiently.

"But why couldn't you have been like the other girls in the street? What did you have to take up with a Mick for?"

"Oh, Ma, cut it out. We've been through all this before. Look, I'm sorry if I've upset you, but you upset me first. I can't help it if I can't give you a bedroom. I haven't got one."

Mrs Jackson's lip wavered. "I wanted something better for you. There's no crime in that."

"And I'm going to get something better," cried Sadie gaily. "One of these days ..."

"We always gave you the best, Sadie. Your da would have worked twenty hours a day to provide for you and Tommy. You had a nice wee home and plenty of food. When I think ..." Now that Mrs Jackson was in full spate again she lifted her head and straightened her back. She began to recall old party dresses of Sadie's, outfits she'd bought her and her brother Tommy for Twelfth of July parades, food she'd cooked on special occasions. Their house might have been small, terraced and a back-to-back, but inside it shone like a palace. You could have eaten off the floor, if you had wanted to.

"I know all that," said Sadie, "but this is my life now."

She got up and finished the dishes. Her mother sat and stared out of the window. Sadie sighed. She might have known it would be like this but she had hoped it would be different. It was as if a pattern was set for them, a way of reacting to another, and they could not break it. She dried the plates, stacked them away, put the broken cup in the bucket.

"Are you for staying then?" she asked. "I'd like you to."

Mrs Jackson looked around. "Aye, I'll stay. I might as well now I'm here."

Chapter Three

BILL WAS sitting on the edge of the pavement with the engine of his motor bike in pieces in front of him.

"Hi, Kevin!" He pushed a lump of hair back from his face with the edge of a grease-smeared hand. "I'm having a terrible job with this thing."

"Let's have a look then." Kevin squatted down.

He worked for an hour, completely absorbed; Bill passed nuts and bolts and spanners. At the end of it, Kevin had found the fault and was well on the way to sorting it.

"You're brilliant," said Bill, who was hopeless with anything mechanical. It was Kitty who had to do the odd jobs in their outfit. She had gone to an evening class on house maintenance last winter. She had come out to watch them and was standing now in the doorway with the baby sitting astride her hip.

"You could do to take a lesson or two from Kevin," she said to her husband.

"I'd never be any use and well you know it. Thanks a lot, Kevin."

"Ah sure, I enjoyed it. You know I like messing around with things." The neighbours brought their radio and television sets to him when they broke down for he had done a bit of radio engineering in his time.

"You should get yourself a bike."

Kevin shrugged. He wiped his hands on a rag and joined Bill on the kerb. He would like a motor bike very much but he had no money for things like that. Bill knew it and said no more.

"I'll go and make some coffee," said Kitty. "Here, hold David." She dumped the boy on his father's lap.

The sun was on their side of the street. It warmed their faces and made the chrome on Bill's bike shine.

As Kevin turned to take his mug of coffee from Kitty he saw a face looking out from his own window. It must be his mother-in-law's. It moved away smartly. Kevin grinned.

"Would Sadie and her mother like a cup, do you think?" asked Kitty.

"I think it might be best to leave well alone in there at the moment," said Kevin. "It's like trying to walk over a nest of hornets without getting stung."

Kitty brought out a chair and sat on the pavement beside them with David on her lap. Two Paradise children were playing close by with a rubber tyre; they were quiet, involved with the thick black ring.

"No kids squalling," said Bill. "Amazing." He stretched and yawned. "It's nice and warm too."

"The street isn't half bad when the sun's shining," said Kevin.

"Come on and I'll take you for a spin," said Bill when they had finished their coffee.

He had a spare crash helmet which he gave to Kevin. "Don't be late for your lunch now," called Kitty as they zoomed off.

"Women!" shouted Bill over the top of the engine's roar.

It was a marvellous day for a motor bike: the sun was bright and golden, the air keen but not cold, and the colours were wild, as if someone had gone crazy with a box of paints. They went through one of the Mersey Tunnels and over into the Wirral. It was a residential area mainly but with lots of green open spaces; it was an expensive place to live and not for the likes of Kevin and Bill. But they could drive through it and enjoy it.

Red, golden, orange, brown, mustard, fawn: the range of colour dazzled Kevin's eye as they whisked past. He wished that Sadie could have been with them, she enjoyed getting out so much, and most of the time she was stuck in those two rooms. If only he could bring her and the baby here to live! The wee fellow needed sun and fresh air and good things to grow up with. It would be fine if they could live in a place like this. Nice houses, trim gardens, roses blooming, children cycling on pavements, cars standing in driveways—sometimes two—men washing and polishing them, picture windows, bright new rooms beyond. It was like a different world. Kevin felt no bitterness towards these people in their comfortable houses with their cars and boats but he did feel a touch of envy, he couldn't help it. He was only human after all, he told himself, and grinned.

They went right across the peninsula to the Dee coast. There were boats out on the estuary, their sails shining against the water. They got off the bike and sat on a wall. On the other side of the estuary was Wales, and beyond that, though not to be seen, Ireland. Terrible place though it was at the moment, Kevin knew he would never forget it. One day, when it was peaceful and people on both sides could tolerate the other without hatred eating into them like a knife, he and Sadie would go back. They had talked about it often, and they were agreed upon that. It might be years, even ten, but some day, yes, some day, they would pack up, take their children and go home.

"What's eating you, Kevin lad?" asked Bill. "You're awful serious looking."

"I was thinking of my mother-in-law," said Kevin, pulling a face and making Bill laugh. "It's better when we have the Irish Sea between us. We only met this morning but I could tell by the look in her eye she didn't fancy me!"

They jumped on the bike and set off again, driving close to the coast, going as far as Neston, a shrimp fishing port. They bought a quarter of shrimps and walked along the front eating them. Kevin decided that he would bring Sadie and Brendan here; they could come on the train and carry a picnic with them and have a long day in the fresh air. They'd do it as soon as Mrs Jackson left.

The pubs were opening. Time for a beer, said Bill. And then they drove back to Liverpool again.

Mrs Jackson was sitting at the table waiting for her lunch. Sadie's face was hot and red as she bent over the pot on the stove. Kevin nodded at his mother-in-law and sat down opposite her. Sadie dished out three platefuls of Irish stew.

"Wee one sleeping?" asked Kevin.

Sadie nodded.

They began to eat. Kevin eyed his mother-in-law from time to time, looking away as soon as she looked at him. Sadie prattled about Brendan. She said she thought she could start trying solids.

"He's far too young," said Mrs Jackson.

"Not nowadays—" began Sadie.

Mrs Jackson sniffed.

"More stew, ma?" asked Sadie.

"No thanks." She folded her arms.

"I'll have some, thanks, Sadie." Kevin held out his plate. "It's great."

"Could have done with a bit more salt, Sadie," said Mrs Jackson. "But it wasn't bad, I must say."

"I didn't think it needed salt," said Kevin.

"Are you going to the football, Kev?" asked Sadie.

Kevin nodded.

"It's a great life for some," said Mrs Jackson.

"He likes going to the football on a Saturday," said Sadie. "Less harm than going to the Lodge."

Now Mrs Jackson bristled. She and Sadie embarked on an argument about the Loyal Orange Lodges. Sadie said they were breeding grounds of prejudice and there would never be peace in Ireland until they were disbanded. Mrs Jackson almost choked at the idea. To think of destroying an institution that had existed for nearly three hundred years to protect all that they held dear from the Catholics! And then she remembered that her son-in-law was a Catholic, one of the enemy that her husband was constantly on the alert against, and she turned a dark shade of red. Kevin ate his stew quickly.

Sadie got up and served the pudding. "Apple pie, ma?"

"Just a little. I haven't much of a tooth for sweet stuff, you know."

Sadie laid a sliver on the plate and passed it to her mother. She cut an enormous wedge for Kevin.

"You've a good appetite, Kevin," said Mrs Jackson. It was the first time she had said his name.

"He's a big man," said Sadie, her voice still sharp.

Kevin ate his pie quickly.

"Cup of tea, Ma?"

"Wouldn't say no. It'd wash the pie down."

The kettle was steaming. Sadie made tea, watched by her mother and husband. She poured three cups, sat down again. Kevin drank his tea, scalding his throat, but not minding about that.

A motor bike roared into life outside, a horn blared.

"That'll be Bill." Kevin leapt up as if a pistol had been fired for the start of a race. He kissed Sadie's cheek. "See you later, Mrs Jackson."

"It's just as well I came," he heard his mother-in-law saying as he left. "You must have been needing some company."

He jumped on the back of Bill's bike.

The match was a good one. Both teams were on form, and Liverpool won! The sun shone throughout, the terraces were packed, and Kevin and Bill enjoyed every moment. They stopped off at the pub on the way back for a celebration drink, talking non-stop, replaying every move of the game. They stayed longer than usual in the pub.

"Lord, it's nearly seven o'clock," said Kevin, noticing the time at last. "I'll be late for my tea."

"Ah, Sadie won't kill you this once," said Bill.

"It's her mother," said Kevin gloomily. "She's got me written off as the worst husband this side of the Irish Sea."

Sadie and her mother had finished their tea when he arrived home, and had a visitor. The priest.

Father Sullivan sat in an armchair beaming. He was from County Monaghan, he was telling Mrs Jackson. Did she know it? No, she informed him, snapping her lips together. She sat as far back in her chair as she could as if she expected that any minute he might jump forward and seize her. It was the first time that she had ever sat in the same room as a Roman Catholic priest and she looked frightened almost to death. Kevin wanted to groan aloud. He would have asked Father Sullivan to stay out of the way if he had thought about it. He glanced over at Sadie and was relieved to see that a little smile was lurking round her lips. She was enjoying herself. Devil that she was! Kevin grinned, then changed his expression quickly as Father Sullivan turned to him.

"I'm delighted to make the acquaintance of your mother-in-law, Kevin. You never hold me she was coming."

"It was unexpected."

"Terrible things are happening in our country are they not, Mrs Jackson?" said the priest. She seemed incapable of answering; her eyes bulged. He went on, "If only a few more were like Sadie and Kevin here, able to show they can live together in peace and harmony!"

Mrs Jackson made a noise in her throat, as if she were being strangled.

"Another cup of tea, Father?" asked Sadie.

"No, I'll need to be getting on. It's two weeks on Sunday young Brendan's to be christened, isn't that right?" He got up, offered his hand to Mrs Jackson who took it, like one hypnotised. "Goodbye, Mrs Jackson, it's been a pleasure to meet you."

Kevin showed him out and wished he could walk off along the street with him and not come back, not until Sadie's mother went away. Her voice was filling the room as he shut the front door.

"What would your da say, Sadie Jackson? Honest to God, I've never been through such an ordeal in my life."

"Don't talk so daft, Ma. You've had bombs exploding all round you for the last few years and you're carrying on like a nut just because a priest has been speaking to you."

Mother and daughter raged at one another, to and fro, accusing one another of stupidity, heartlessness, lack of respect, mindlessness. Kevin stood at the back of the room helplessly. Sadie had a dreadful tongue on her when she got going, he had felt the blast of it himself on many occasions. She was like a demon possessed, not caring how far she went. And her mother was dredging up crimes of Sadie's that stretched back almost to the day she was born. And every time Sadie blasted back at her she hugged her arms around her chest and moaned, like a woman keening at a wake, and said, "What would your da say?"

In the end Sadie blew herself out, like a storm. She came to rest standing by the window; her mother sat with her hands over her eyes. There was silence in the room.

"I'll be leaving then," said Mrs Jackson.

"You're too late for tonight's boat," said Sadie. "And there isn't one on Sunday." She took a deep breath. "I'm sorry, Ma, I didn't mean to fly at you like that but you do go on about things!"

Mrs Jackson removed her hands from her face. She did not look quite ready yet for a reconciliation though Kevin had a feeling that she would allow herself to be brought round. Unfortunately for him!

"It was very upsetting for me to have a priest walking in like that," she said in a low voice. "It gave me a queer fright. I've never had anything to do with them and I never will again, you can be sure of that."

"But he didn't bite you."

"You can't trust them."

"O.K., we won't have him in again while you're here, not if you're going to have a fit like that."

Mrs Jackson sniffed.

Kevin glanced at the table to see if they had left him any food. He was ravenous, after all the fresh air and beer, but it would not be a good idea to ask for his tea right now in the middle of all this upheaval.

"Are you staying then, Ma?" asked Sadie.

"I suppose I'll have to," said her mother. "Seeing as there are no boats."

There'll be one on Monday, Kevin wanted to say.

"Are you hungry, Kev?"

"Just a bit."

Sadie had kept his meal hot in the oven for him. He sat at the table and ate it whilst his mother-in-law sat at the other side looking the other way. There was nowhere for her to go. And the only way they could get away from her would be to go to bed, but it was a bit early for that yet.

"Let's see what's on the telly." Sadie switched it on.

"So you're having the wee one christened in the Roman church are you?" said Mrs Jackson.

"It's usual," said Sadie, "when one of the parents is a Catholic."

"They make you, don't they?"

"They don't *make* you exactly."

"No, but they'd make it unpleasant if you didn't."

Sadie turned up the volume on the television set. Kevin finished his tea.

"Think I might slip round to the pub for a quick one with Bill. Would you mind, Sadie?"

She glowered at him but did not voice her objection, unwilling to have her mother witness discord between them. Kevin reached for his coat.

"I'll not be late," he said. "See you later, Mrs Jackson."

The pub was warm and full of people enjoying themselves. He pushed his way through until he found Bill. He was playing darts.

"Fancy a game, Kev?"

"Sure would."

At closing time Bill and Kevin emerged. It was seldom they spent a whole evening in the pub. They were in good spirits and began to sing, softly, as they walked home. It was only as they turned into their own street that Kevin remembered his mother-in-law. He stopped singing.

The two women were watching television, their backs stiff, their heads rigid, like two dummies on a set. Sadie's face was blank with annoyance. He bent to kiss her and she drew back, as if he had leprosy.

"Sorry I'm late but I was playing darts with Bill and forgot the time. Will I make the two of you a cup of tea?"

"No thank you," said his mother-in-law.

"No thank you," said his wife.

He sat down behind them and they all gazed at the television set until it closed down for the night. Then they got up and made a bed on the settee carrying in the sheets and blankets from the bedroom quietly so that they would not waken the baby. Mrs Jackson put in her rollers, winding them up tight and spearing them with quick jabs so that Kevin flinched, expecting each time that she would pierce her skull.

"Will you be all right now, Ma?" asked Sadie.

"I'll manage."

They shut the door of their room. They undressed in silence and got into bed.

"I'm sorry, Sadie," said Kevin. "I only had a couple of pints—"

"You were drunk!"

"Don't talk daft. I had two pints. You can ask Bill."

"Shush! You'll waken the baby."

Sadie flipped over on to her side and pulled the blankets round her shoulder. Kevin lay on his back with no covers on his right side. The baby was breathing gently, up and down. Through the wall he heard his mother-in-law turning over and the settee springs twanging, then she groaned and sighed and turned again, and the springs twanged anew. She might as well have been in the same room as them.

He did not know that he could put up with a whole week of it.

Chapter Four

IT RAINED on Sunday, heavily.

"Of all the luck!" moaned Sadie. "And it's been quite nice all week."

Mrs Jackson sat by the window staring out at the rain as if she had expected nothing else. She was a woman who constantly expected the worst from life so was therefore never surprised when she got it. Kevin was reading the paper and had been for two hours. Sadie wanted to scream. She went into the bedroom. Brendan was sleeping like an angel. She leaned over his cot and spoke to him softly.

"People are nothing but a pain in the neck, Brendan boy. Now if there was just the two of us—"

She broke off as the door opened. Kevin came in.

"Would you mind if I slipped out to the pub for a few minutes?"

"The pub! Again! You're never away from the place these days."

"Now that's not true. I don't go very often."

"You were there nearly all day yesterday."

"That was different."

They talked in whispers, mindful of the extra pair of ears in the next room. Sadie knew from experience that her mother could hear what was going on ten streets away.

"You don't seem to care if you leave me alone for hours at a time," said Sadie.

"You're not alone."

"You're the end, Kevin McCoy!"

"Well, she's your mother."

There seemed no answer to that. Sadie sat back on the bed and sighed. Kevin came to her, put his arm round her.

"I'm sorry, love."

"But she's my mother, like you said."

"I'm not blaming you for that!"

They grinned at one another. He kissed her, she snuggled against his shoulder. He felt so warm and solid. They stayed like that for a while enjoying the comfort and warmth of being together. Rain flayed the window panes making the room seem cosier, a refuge from the cold and wet outside.

"I like the sound of rain," murmured Sadie sleepily.

Brendan moved in his cot, flung his hand up above his head. A tremor passed across his face.

"Sure, he must be dreaming," said Kevin.

"I wonder what about?"

"His next feed."

They laughed.

"It's nice having a baby, isn't it?" said Sadie.

"It's not bad. I'm getting used to it."

"You!"

Sadie punched him lightly on the chest.

"Sadie?" They heard Mrs Jackson's voice calling. It sounded querulous.

"Yes, Ma?" Sadie sat up.

"Could I make myself a pot of tea, do you think?" The voice came from just behind the door. "Me throat's dry."

"I'm just coming!" Sadie slid off the bed. "I'll make you one. You go on off to the pub for an hour," she said to Kevin. "Yes, go on! You can't sit in here with my mother all day. It'd drive you round the twist."

Mrs Jackson was looking peeved. She had her hands folded on her lap, feet together, back poker-straight.

Kevin followed Sadie out of the bedroom.

"Are you going round to Mr Fiske's then?" said Sadie. "You promised you would, didn't you, to give him a hand with fixing his telly?"

"Oh yes," said Kevin. "I did that. See you later, Mrs Jackson."

He went quickly.

"He seems to help people fix a lot of things," said Mrs Jackson.

"Aye well he's very handy at doing things. He was learning to be a radio engineer in London. That was before his dad died and he had to go home."

Sadie filled the kettle. The rain showed no sign of stopping.

"I wish I'd brought my knitting with me," said her mother.

"I've got some you could do if you like. I'm making a pram set for Brendan."

"You knitting, Sadie Jackson! I don't believe it."

Sadie fetched the polythene bag in which she kept her wool. It was a glorious tangle inside and gave her mother plenty to tut over and something to do sorting it out. She rolled up the balls of wool, examined the battered patterns, shook her head and exclaimed over Sadie's ineptness. Then she began to knit, her fingers moving deftly, the wool flying under them, dazzling Sadie's eyes. She would never be able to knit like that.

Brendan woke; Sadie brought him into the kitchen to feed him.

"He's a lovely looking baby," said Mrs Jackson.

Sadie looked up at her mother and smiled. "Yes, he is, isn't he?"

And suddenly everything was all right between them. They were in tune with one another, united over their admiration of this small child and over the tie that existed between them too. Sadie had not often felt this way with her mother before, at ease, both of them doing things, contented. It would not last, not all week, that would be too much to hope for, what with her mother's need to attack everything and her own hot temper, but whilst it did it made her feel warm and happy.

Kevin came in looking apprehensive and was startled by the peace in the room.

"Ma's knitting Brendan a coat," said Sadie. "She's a great knitter. Sure he'll look like a king when she's done with him."

"Well, I'm not too bad with the ould needles," said Mrs Jackson.

"I thought maybe Ma'd like a wee drop of that port you bought her, Kevin. A wee drink before Sunday dinner."

"It's not the right thing to drink before dinner," said Kevin, opening the cupboard door and lifting out the bottle.

"I don't mind," said Mrs Jackson. "I don't expect you to have a cocktail bar you know."

She drank two glasses of port and became a little skittish.

"It's not often I touch the stuff, mind! Sadie'll tell you that, Kevin. I keep a drop in the parlour for when I'm feeling poorly. It revives me when I get a touch of faintness."

She praised Sadie's cooking over dinner. "She's not a bad wee cook is she, Kevin? She must have picked up more from me than I thought. In fact you're a right lucky man to have her!"

"Ma!" said Sadie. "I never thought I'd see the day when I'd hear you saying that."

"No, neither did I," admitted Mrs Jackson. "You've come on a bit in the last year or two. Dear but you were terrible when you were younger!" Mrs Jackson shook her head. "You were far worse than your brother Tommy."

"How is Tommy? Have you heard?"

He'd gone to Australia, and the last his mother heard of him was doing well. He was not much of a letter writer.

"It's terrible having the two of you so far away. Only your da and I left now." Mrs Jackson sighed. "And all that trouble round us."

"Come on, Ma, don't think of that now," said Sadie. "Forget Belfast for a while. You're on your holidays."

"I wish your da was here too."

Sadie was not sure of that: he was a peaceable enough man in his way, made less noise than her mother but he was staunch in his Orange beliefs, had a real hatred of Catholics, and she could not imagine him sitting easily with Kevin. Her mother felt strongly too but her desire to be with her daughter and grandson had overruled her prejudice.

After lunch Kevin said that he would mind the baby and Sadie and her mother could go out. The rain had stopped. They took the train to the Wirral and walked along the coast looking at the boats as Kevin had done with Bill the day before. Mrs Jackson's feet were hurting so they could not walk too far. They found a tea shop and had a pot of tea and a plate of home-made scones with thick plum jam.

"I must say it's nice to be able to get out without worrying about people shooting or throwing bombs," said Mrs Jackson. "It's a desperate strain on the nerves, Sadie." She stirred her tea. "It's not often I bother going out now at all. Well, it's not worth it is it? And every time your da goes for a drink me heart's jumping like mad in case there's a bomb in the pub."

"I want you to have a real good holiday this week, Ma. We'll do lots of things together and Kevin'll keep Brendan one evening and we'll go to the pictures."

Sadie asked Kitty to come in for a cup of coffee the following morning. "And meet me ma," she added, rolling her eyes. "Ach, she's not half bad. But you know what mothers are!"

Mrs Jackson seemed to like Kitty. She admired David and said he was big for his age.

Kitty was excited about something. There was a wee smile jumping about her lips and she kept looking out of the window with a kind of far-away expression. In the end she had to come out with it.

"Oh, Sadie, you'll never guess! Bill said I was to say nothing just yet but—"

"What's happening?"

"He applied for another job a week or two back and now he's been called for an interview on Friday."

"Is it a good position then?" asked Mrs Jackson.

"Sales representative for a chemical firm."

"Sounds all right." Mrs Jackson looked over at Sadie. *Better than labouring*. The words were in her eyes.

"Of course he might not get it," said Kitty, but she smiled.

"In Liverpool?" asked Sadie.

"No, Manchester."

"Manchester," echoed Sadie bleakly. "But you wouldn't move there would you?"

"He'd have to. Don't look so glum, Sadie! He hasn't got the job yet."

When Kitty had gone Mrs Jackson said, "Nice girl that. Sounds like her husband is a real go-ahead fella too."

Sadie stuck out her bottom lip, said nothing.

There was a tap on the door and then it opened. Maria put her head round it.

"Sadie," she said and stopped, seeing Mrs Jackson.

"Come in, Maria, and meet my mother."

Maria had her two youngest sisters with her, Crystal and Donna. They all came in. Donna staggered across to Mrs Jackson and laid one sticky hand on her knee. Mrs Jackson tried to smile. Maria pulled the child away, apologising. There was a greasy spot left on the knee of Mrs Jackson's new blue jersey wool dress, bought just the week before, for her holiday.

"Mam's not well. I had to stay and mind the babies." Mrs Paradise was often not well; if it wasn't her stomach, it was her kidneys or her throat. Maria was frequently at home.

"What's up with your mother then, Maria?"

"Oh she's not been well recently, what with worrying over Gabriel and then Saturday night she was real annoyed with Michael and Anthony. They went to the car park at the Phil after she'd told them not to and I had to go out looking for them."

"The Phil?" said Mrs Jackson. "What in the name is that?"

"The Liverpool Philharmonic," said Sadie. "The orchestra."

"What were they doing at the car park?"

"They guide in the motorists in the hopes of getting a tip."

"But why should they? It's a free park, is it?"

"Well, maybe the motorists might be a bit worried what'd happen to their cars if they didn't tip."

Mrs Jackson nodded her head slowly. "I see. An extortion racket, eh?"

"It's a kind of fancy name for it," said Sadie.

"My mother doesn't allow them to go," put in Maria quickly. "She does not approve."

Mrs Jackson continued to nod her head knowingly.

"It's not very nice, Ma, but the kids are up to worse things at home, you must admit that."

Mrs Jackson was not prepared to admit anything; she sniffed, fell silent and eyed Maria's small sisters. Donna was restless and attracted by the bright blue dress; Crystal was fretful, in the midst of cutting teeth. Maria soon got up to go.

"Fancy names they've all got," said Mrs Jackson, dabbing at the spot on her dress with a dampened handkerchief. "Gabriel! And Crystal!"

"I expect Mrs Paradise needs something fancy in her life."

"Aye you're right there. How many are there?"

"Seven."

"Seven! It's no wonder they can hardly keep body and soul together. No woman should have seven children."

"Well, she has them now."

"That's obvious enough. Are you friendly with them, like?"

"Yes. Why, what's the matter?"

"I never said a word."

"You don't like them being black, do you? Oh, you make me sick at times! Everyone would need to be white, Protestant and Unionist to please you. You're as narrow-minded as—" Sadie spluttered and was lost for words. Fury burned in her. Why did her mother have to go and spoil everything just when they were getting on nicely? Then she shrugged. Her mother would never change now.

"I don't know what you had to fly off the handle at me for," said her mother. "I don't have to like people if I don't want to, do I?"

Sadie conceded that she did not.

Mrs Jackson liked Mrs Hignett well enough. Every time they went into the shop Mrs Jackson parked herself on the high chair beside the counter and had a good gossip. They talked about food prices and the country going downhill until Sadie's legs were tired with standing. She did not tell her mother that Mrs Hignett was a Catholic and Mrs Jackson never did find out.

"Pleasant wee woman that," she said.

It was on Wednesday morning that Kevin got his letter from Tyrone and cracked his mother-in-law's false teeth. Sadie did not hear what was in the letter until after her mother had gone back to Belfast but she heard about the teeth straightaway. They were not in her mother's mouth when Kevin cracked them; they had been in a tumbler of cleaning fluid on the draining board. Kevin, distressed by the contents of his letter, had not looked properly at the contents of the tumbler. He had thought it was just some old water and picking it up, had tipped it into the porcelain sink.

Sadie came through from the bedroom to find her mother holding the sides of her head and moaning sorely.

"My teeth, my teeth! Kevin's broken my teeth."

Both plates, holding the top and bottom dentures, were cracked right across.

"You must have tossed them in with some force," said Sadie.

"I never knew they were there," said Kevin. His mother-in-law looked as if she would never believe that.

"What am I going to do without my teeth?" moaned Mrs Jackson. "I'll not be able to go out. I wouldn't be seen dead in the street without them. Not even this street!"

Kevin had to go to work. There was nothing more he could do now, said Sadie, so there was no point in him losing a day's wages into the bargain.

Sadie was left with her mother and the damaged teeth. They glared up at her from the draining board, pink and white and shiny, and cracked.

"I'll just have to take them to the dentist."

"They'll take years to fix them."

"We'll see about that," said Sadie.

She left Brendan with her mother and set off with the teeth in a box. She had a nice dentist who had looked after her teeth when she was expecting Brendan but she knew he was busy and she had always had to make appointments weeks in advance.

The receptionist was not particularly interested or bothered about her mother's teeth. "She's not our patient after all. And the mechanics are dead busy. Excuse me." The phone was ringing and she had other things to do. The queue in the waiting room was enormous and they were one dentist short. He was off to Morocco on holiday, the receptionist said. Lucky him!

Sadie wandered up the corridor when the receptionist's attention was diverted. She hovered outside Mr Carson's door. She heard the whir of a drill, then a clinking noise, then water running. She kept her eye on the end of the corridor for the appearance of a white coat, ready to dive into the toilet next door if necessary.

A dental nurse came by. "Can I help you?"

"No, no thanks. I'm waiting for a friend."

At last Mr Carson's door opened and out he came with a patient.

"If you'd just give your card to the receptionist," he said.

Sadie signalled to him. "Mr Carson, could I have a word with you please? It's desperately important. A real emergency, you might say. Life or death, that kind of thing."

"Have you toothache, Mrs McCoy?"

The receptionist came up the corridor and saw Sadie. "Now, Mrs McCoy—"

"Worse than that," said Sadie to Mr Carson. "Much worse."

"Come in for a minute then," he said.

When she emerged ten minutes later she bumped into the receptionist's starched front.

"Well?"

"He said to come back at five, he'd see they were done for me."

The receptionist shook her head.

"Well, after I told him about my mother and my husband, and her being all funny about him being a Catholic, he said he'd have to do his bit to help diplomatic relations along."

"I might have known you'd talk your way round anything."

But the receptionist smiled. And Sadie ran home singing and laughing to herself. She had to put up with one day of her mother moaning and groaning but it could have been worse, though of course Mrs Jackson never let her son-in-law forget it, even after she had the teeth back in her mouth.

The week moved on. Kevin spent more time in the pub than he had in all the months they had lived in Liverpool. In the daytime Sadie and her mother walked Brendan in his pram. They went through the parks. "Not a bad lot of parks, I must say," said Mrs Jackson. They looked at the big houses that backed on to them, where once rich merchants had lived, but which now were used as hotels or were broken into flats. They walked round the streets and Mrs Jackson saw some that reminded her of home, rows of terraced houses all spruced up with coloured paint around their doors and windows, fancy curtains, scoured and polished front steps.

"Pity you couldn't get one of these, Sadie."

"We've no money."

Mrs Jackson sighed.

On her last night, she and Sadie were alone together. Kevin had gone to play in a darts match. Sadie poured her mother the last drop of port.

"I'm glad you came, Ma. It was nice having you here. And I'm glad you met Kevin, too."

"Aye." Mrs Jackson didn't sound so sure.

"You like Kevin don't you?"

"Oh yes. It's just—oh well, Sadie, it'd have been easier—"

"Look, I know all that," said Sadie patiently.

"It's not just him being a Catholic. But he's not got much of a job either, he can't give you the kind of home I'd like you to have."

"It doesn't matter."

"It does, Sadie. You're a fine looking girl, you could have had lots of boys."

"I didn't want them."

"But just think of your kids growing up Catholics and you not one of them. You'll be the odd man out." Sadie was silent, for that did bother her. Her mother went on, "The priest'll try to set them against you or make you turn too. Can you imagine your own childer set against you? I tell you, Sadie, it'll never work in the long run. Oh it's all right now maybe, the wee fellow's just a baby and not knowing anything but when he's bigger ... What he'll think of you then, his Protestant mother?"

"I don't know. We'll have to wait and see."

Mrs Jackson spoke softly now. "Sadie, do you think you're doing the right thing? Staying with Kevin I mean? Oh he's a nice enough lad but he seems over fond of a drink, does he not? There's other lads with steady jobs ... You're young ... nineteen ... too young to throw everything away. You could come home with me ... you and the baby—"

"Come home with you? To Belfast?"

"There's your old room. And Brendan could have Tommy's when he's big enough."

"I don't want to go home. Ma, I'm staying with Kevin. For good. No matter how bad things get at times." Sadie was horrified at her mother's suggestion.

"You're daft then." Mrs Jackson sat back, her lips set tight again.

"I love him."

Mrs Jackson sniffed.

Chapter Five

SADIE AND Kevin waited until the boat sailed. They stood on the pier watching it move out into the dark river, lights gleaming, siren blaring. They thought of it crossing the Irish Sea and berthing in the morning in Belfast Lough.

They turned their backs on it and walked away.

"It wasn't so bad having, Ma," said Sadie.

"No," said Kevin, and then he grinned. "I'm glad she's gone though." He took Sadie's hand.

"So am I," said Sadie fervently.

Maria was looking after Brendan so they had the evening to themselves. They went to the cinema and afterwards bought fish and chips to eat as they walked home.

"Kevin," said Sadie, gulping down a hot vinegary chip, "do you think Brendan will turn against me when he's older? For not being Catholic?"

"Of course not. I wouldn't let him, would I? What rubbish has your mother been filling your head with? You're full of crazy ideas about the Catholic faith. You're always suspecting there's some big conspiracy to get everyone into the fold."

"Well, isn't there?" she said seriously.

"Nut!" He tousled her hair affectionately.

She said no more, not wanting to spoil their evening, but her mother's words haunted her. But there was nothing to be done, not that Sadie could see, for take Kevin's religion she could not. It was an accident of fate that they had not been born into the same faith and it was something she must accept, that she did accept, and had done, more or less, from the beginning. She grinned to herself. In the beginning she had certainly accepted it, thus placing him firmly in the enemy camp.

"Wee spot of trouble up ahead," said Kevin. "Let's nip round the corner."

Some youths were roaming the street further along. Sadie and Kevin could spot trouble of that sort a mile away: they had seen it too much at home. Sadie did not like walking these streets late at night. Once she would not have bothered, she had seldom been afraid, but now she was more conscious of her own safety. It came from having a kid, Kitty said, you felt you had to protect yourself because of him. You couldn't be carefree any more! There were a lot of things to adapt to when you had a child. It changed your life in all sorts of ways that Sadie had never thought about before.

As they neared their own street they saw a huge fire blazing on a piece of waste ground ahead. All over Liverpool there was waste ground where the bulldozers had ground down the old decaying houses. One day their street might go too. A car was alight. It was an old one that had been lying abandoned for months. Kids danced round it outlined by the flickering light of the flames.

"Looks like a couple of Paradises are there," said Kevin.

Maria was listening to the radio when they got in. "Wee one's asleep," she said. "He's been as good as gold."

They paid her for baby-sitting, not very much for they had little to spare, but always something. She never wanted to take it but they insisted that she did, and spend it on herself.

"O.K.," she said. "I promise. Good-night, Sadie. Good-night, Kevin."

"She'll be off out again in five minutes looking for her brothers," said Sadie. "She's far too good-natured. I don't know how she does it. Cup of tea, Kev?"

"Wouldn't mind."

It was nice to have had an evening out and then sit drinking a cup of tea and talking.

"Did you ever see anything like Ma's face when you cracked her teeth?" Sadie laughed until tears came to her eyes.

It was then that Kevin remembered that he still had to tell Sadie about the contents of his letter. He sobered.

"Sadie, do you mind the letter I got? There's something I have to tell you."

"What's wrong? Is it serious?"

"It's Gerald."

She relaxed a bit. Gerald was Kevin's seventeen-year-old brother, and could have little to do with her. A wild wayward boy, he had been in trouble ever since the current unrest had started in Ireland.

"Seems he's in bad trouble. My mother was a bit vague about it, she didn't say what exactly. She was upset of course. She says she can't cope with him any more."

Sadie frowned, waited.

"She says he'll need to get out of Ireland."

"So?"

"She wants to send him over here."

"How do you mean over here?"

"To Liverpool."

"To you?"

"Yes."

"But she can't. Not to stay. I mean, I know my mother's been here for a week but—"

"I'm his brother, Sadie."

"And the head of the family?" she said sarcastically.

"Yes. Gerald needs help. I can't turn my back on him. He's in a terrible state, my mother says. And she's nearly out of her wits."

"And I'll be out of mine if we have him here."

"We'll have to have him."

"Are you serious?" Sadie spluttered. "You're going to have him *here*, in this place, to live with us?"

"Just in the meantime. Not for good."

44

"I'm glad to hear that! I thought you might want him to live with us till death do us part."

"Oh be quiet, Sadie." Kevin held his head between his hands. "I don't know what to do."

"But do you think you'll be able to cope with him when your mother couldn't? You've said yourself the two of you didn't get on together."

"Yes, but—"

"Yes, I know: he's your brother." Sadie calmed. "Flesh and blood and all that. Oh, I suppose he's got to come." She sighed, refilled their cups.

"He may not stay very long."

"He may not come at all. If I were him I wouldn't. After all, he's turned seventeen now and can fend for himself."

The next day being Sunday, and Kevin not having to go to work, he wrote to his mother. After Sadie had cleared the breakfast dishes from the table he sat down and addressed himself to the task. He sat for a long time over the letter, chewing the end of the biro, scratching his head, making two false starts and crumpling the mauve-coloured pages which Sadie had seen in Mrs Hignett's shop and fancied. Every time she bought a writing pad she got a different colour. "What have you this time?" Kevin would ask. He only wrote to his mother and she would not mind what colour of paper his letters came on, so long as they came. He thought of his mother standing in the kitchen starting on a mound of ironing, straightening her tired back, sighing a little as she lifted the first shirt and spread it over the board. During his childhood his mother had been a patient, uncomplaining woman, complaining too little perhaps, for everyone had thought she was as strong and willing as a horse and heaped chores upon her without question; but since his father's death she had changed, become difficult, querulous, and bitter. Kevin could not blame her. She'd had a hard life. And then to have her man blown up at a time when she should have been able to take things more easily!

Kevin jettisoned another page. Everything he wrote was not what he really wanted to say. Finally, he wrote: "Send

Gerald over. I will look after him and get him a job. Don't worry. Enclose P.O. for fare. Hope you are all well. Love Kevin."

Don't worry! Easy words to write. She would worry: it was part of her nature. She would worry when Gerald was gone, but less than if he was there.

"I'm just going up to see Bill for a minute, Sadie."

Sadie's face fell. "You're not going out to the pub again?"

"No, honest I'm not. I'm only wanting a word with Bill. About the darts match."

He went up the stairs to Bill's flat. He was going to borrow money for Gerald's fare. Sadie would raise the ceiling if she knew. There were things it was better that she did not know at times. Money causes a lot of trouble, thought Kevin bitterly, too much, for it didn't seem important in itself. But if you hadn't enough then life was a struggle. As it had been for his mother. It mustn't be the same for Sadie. It was up to him to see that it wasn't.

Kitty had gone out for a walk with David but Bill was at home. Of course he could lend Kevin the money.

"Think nothing of it. Only too glad to help out." He opened his wallet.

"I can pay you back next week."

"Any time. Not to worry. I'm flush at the moment. Just had some unexpected commission."

Kevin hesitated. "I'd be grateful if you didn't say anything to Kitty. You see she might let slip to Sadie, and Sadie'd do her nut if she knew I was paying Gerald's fare."

"Not a word," promised Bill.

They went out then to the pub. Bill suggested it, and Kevin felt he could not refuse, under the circumstances. He drank his beer guiltily, not enjoying it, thinking all the while of Sadie.

The next day he bought a postal order and posted the letter to his mother.

And the next day Bill got a letter offering him the job in Manchester.

Kitty ran downstairs to tell Sadie. She was bubbling over with excitement.

"Guess?" she cried, but Sadie did not need to.

"That's great, Kitty. I'm very pleased for you." She was bathing Brendan in a plastic bath in front of the fire and had lost the soap somewhere in amongst the water. She chased it round the bath, holding Brendan with her other hand. He was annoyed by the interruption in his bathing routine and began to squall.

"We're going to try to buy our own house," said Kitty. "We've been saving for ages."

Sadie found the soap. It was slithery from having been in the water. "Oh, do be quiet," she said to Brendan.

"Bill's getting a car with the job."

"That's marvellous."

"We'll be able to come through and take you and Kevin and Brendan out."

"We'd like that."

Sadie rinsed Brendan off quickly, lifted him so that his heels were clean of the water and shook him gently to get rid of surplus moisture. He yelled. He hated going into the bath and he hated coming out. "Dear but he's perverse! Just like all men."

"My mother said she'd help us out. She's a widow you know, but she's got a wee bit put by. She's offered to pay the lawyer and she's going to give us some furniture."

"That's great." Sadie proceeded to dry and powder Brendan.

"Oh Sadie, cheer up, love! It's not far away. We'll see you often."

"But not like this. Not every day. Dropping in. Saturday nights. Meeting in the street, at the shop, walking in the park. Oh I'm sorry, Kitty. I don't want to sound mean about it. I am glad for you, really."

"Look, I must go," said Kitty. "I've left David sleeping. I'll see you after, Sadie."

Sadie dressed and fed Brendan, thinking of Kitty and Bill taking off for their new prosperity whilst she and Kevin would stick forever in this grisly street with water running down the wall of their bedroom and listen to the mice scrabbling at nights and their son would grow up to be a juvenile delinquent. Ah shut up, Sadie McCoy, sure you let your mind run on in the daftest way once it gets going!

"Don't ever pay too much heed to your ma," she told Brendan. "I'm really the luckiest girl alive to have you and your dad. Who cares about a bit of damp and no bath? Ha, ha!"

She ran her finger down the wallpaper and watched the water run. That was really bad for a child, her mother had said; he'd get bronchitis, weak lungs, pneumonia, and she and Kevin would have rheumatism and weak chests before they were much older. Sadie grinned. Her mother was a real prophet of doom if ever there was one! Not that she probably wasn't right in what she said. But there didn't seem to be much choice for them, not at the moment.

She took Brendan for a walk, to get out of the house. She pushed his pram into the town past the place where she knew Kevin was working. He was employed on a site where a block of offices was being built.

She saw him at once, picked him out easily. "There's your da," she said to the sleeping Brendan. "That handsome guy with the black hair."

Kevin put down his shovel and came to meet them. "Anything up?"

"Just felt like seeing you. Don't know why, I'm sure. But there it is."

He grinned. He looked healthy and tanned from working in the open air, and the muscles of his arms were strong from the work.

"Doing anything after work tonight?" asked Sadie.

"Sure am. Got a date."

"Oh?"

"With a blonde. Fiery temper she's got when she's roused! But she's all right. In fact, I really fancy her quite a lot." They stood smiling at one another for a minute or two and then Kevin said, "I'd better be getting back or the gaffer'll be after me. Don't want to get my books."

"Give me a kiss before you go then."

He kissed her and a chorus of whistles rose up from the site.

"Ach, they're jealous," said Kevin. "And no wonder?"

Cheered, Sadie walked home. She went up to Kitty's and said again that she was really pleased for them having such good luck, and this time she meant it.

"I'll miss you too, you know, Sadie. We'll have to get together at week-ends."

"We'll do that," said Sadie.

Life was always shifting. Well, so be it, there was nothing you could do about it anyway. And one day it would shift again for her and Kevin; she need only have faith.

She would need to have a lot of faith in a lot of different ways, she thought, as she stood in church on Sunday watching her baby being christened Brendan Kevin McCoy by Father Sullivan. She would need to have faith in Kevin that he would see her through where their children and religion were concerned. She looked up at his dark head, the strong line of his jaw, his straight back. He was a good man to have faith in.

Maria was godmother and a friend of Kevin's at work, Michael Quinn, fellow-Irishman, was godfather. Sadie stood by feeling like an onlooker. She was the outsider here; the ceremony seemed to have little to do with her. It was only the second time she had been in a Catholic church. The first time was when she and Kevin had got married. The smell of incense and the flickering of candles made her uneasy, as did the statues of the Virgin Mary and the other saints. She knew it was due to prejudice, Kevin had told her so many times; she knew it in her mind, tried to talk to herself sternly, calling herself a stupid eejit, but it bothered her nevertheless. She was on edge the whole time, nervous as a cat, jumping when the priest looked at her, even though she knew him well and did not mind him in her own kitchen. But, from as far back as she could remember, the Catholic church was a place of evil to her, a place she should never enter lest the evil spirits got hold of her.

Who's the good man? King Billy!
Who's the bad man?
The Pope!
If I'd a penny
Do you know what I'd do?
I'd hang the Pope
And let King Billy through.

The jingle ran through her head. She started guiltily as if they could all see inside her head and read her mind. The priest was blessing the baby and now they were all crossing themselves, her husband, Maria, and Michael Quinn.

Brendan wouldn't sing the songs she'd sung. Nor would he sing the songs that Kevin had sung. Or would he? No, he must not. He must find his own songs.

"Well, Sadie, you've a fine-looking lad there," said Father Sullivan. "May he bring you lots of joy."

Sadie took her baby and carried him out of the church. Kevin walked behind her smiling.

They had a party when they got home, with Maria and Michael Quinn, and Kitty and Bill; and Mrs Hignett looked in with her neighbour Mrs Fiske, the plumber's wife, to bring presents for Brendan and drink his health, and when Mrs Paradise had an hour to spare she too came bringing three of the younger children with her. Even Mr Paradise stopped off for ten minutes to say hello, although he had had enough of christenings in his time he told Kevin, as he tossed down a glass of wine.

Sadie and Kitty had been busy the day before preparing food. They had made dozens of sandwiches, sausage rolls and other savouries, baked cakes and biscuits and a huge lemon meringue pie, and there were tinned peaches and pears, two bowls of jelly and masses of cream. Kevin had bought sparkling wine which went off with a bang like champagne when he eased off the cork. He shattered the lampshade with one cork and everybody laughed, even Sadie who had bought it only the week before and was rather attached to it.

Michael Quinn had brought his guitar to entertain them. He sang *Phil the Fluter's Ball* and *The Wearing of the Green*. At the end of the latter song he wiped his eyes and declared, "There's no place like the ould place. Up the Republic!"

"Shall I sing *The Sash*?" Sadie asked Kevin. "Just to keep things even?"

"Don't be such a twit! He means nothing by it. He's an Irishman and it's an Irish song. Besides, when the Irish get a glass inside them they're inclined to be sentimental."

"But he knows I'm a Protestant."

"That's not in his mind at all. Now, Sadie, you're not going to start up that nonsense on the day Brendan gets christened, are you?"

"Christened in *your* church though, are you forgetting that? Why do you always have to get things your way? We had to get married in your church too. You wouldn't have got married in mine, would you?"

"My church wouldn't have recognised it. I can't help it, Sadie. That's just the way of it."

"Huh!"

"Look, the wine's making you excited. Maybe you should lay off it."

"Excited, is it?"

"Keep your hair on!"

"What are you two arguing about?" said Kitty, joining them.

"Nothing," said Kevin.

Bill called him and he went, leaving Sadie with Kitty.

"What's up with you?" asked Kitty.

"It's just this business of getting the baby christened a Catholic," said Sadie.

"For goodness sake you've been through all that. I can't see why you make such a big fuss about it. Enjoy yourself!"

Sadie did. Maria borrowed Michael's guitar and she too sang. Her eyes were soft and happy as she plucked the strings. Michael left soon afterwards—he had a date with a girl— and Sadie felt easier when he was gone. Kitty and Bill had brought their record player so they had music, and when Mrs Paradise had drunk a glass of wine she felt in fine voice and gave them a song. A plantation song from Jamaica. She sang well, her low warm voice filling the room and quietening them. A song about a girl who worked on a banana plantation, a black girl, poor and in love.

"Sure I think everybody enjoyed themselves rightly," said Kevin, as they cleared away the debris afterwards and started on the mountain of dishes. "Even you!"

"What do you mean—even me?"

"Well, after all the fuss you were making this morning!"

"I still feel that way you know. Can't help it. But I like it living here far better than I did in London. The people are friendlier. They care if you're alive or dead."

Sadie went to bed happy, but when the postman came in the morning bearing a pink envelope with a Tyrone postmark her mood changed fast.

"What does she say?"

"Wait, wait." Kevin was reading.

Sadie was praying: please don't let him come, please leave us alone.

Kevin lifted his head. "He's coming," he said. "Saturday morning."

Chapter Six

"I WISH they'd stop the boats running altogether between here and Ireland," said Sadie. "And then we might get peace." She sat in her dressing gown drinking a cup of tea watching Kevin get ready to go down to the docks.

"They could still swim across."

"My ma wouldn't though," said Sadie, amused by the notion. "Could you see her purple hat bobbing on the waves? She'd arrive on shore telling us what a terrible crossing she'd had and how she hadn't slept a wink all night and her feet were killing her!"

Kevin buttoned his jacket. "I'd better be off." He hesitated. "Sadie, will you try—?"

"Oh yes, I'll try."

Kevin reached the Pier Head as the passengers from the Belfast boat were coming out of the dock. He saw Gerald, head down, carrying a canvas hold-all. Kevin waved, Gerald crossed the street to join him.

"Have a good trip?"

Gerald shrugged. He put the hold-all by his feet, stuck his hands in his pockets. He did not look at Kevin's face.

"I suppose we might as well head home then," said Kevin. He felt as if someone had planted a stone inside him. It was not fair to take this surly boy home and dump him on Sadie.

But what else could he do? He lifted the bag. "Come on then, Gerald. My goodness, this weighs a ton."

"There are no bombs in it, if that's what's worrying you."

"Hardly. I'm sure you were well searched on your way through."

"You can say that again."

"How's ma?" asked Kevin, on the bus.

"Just the same."

"What does that mean?"

"Moaning and groaning. Always something wrong with her."

"And no wonder!" Kevin flared, then controlled himself. It would not do for him to be losing his temper straightaway with Gerald; that would get them nowhere. He must remember that Gerald had grown into his teens amidst the violence of Belfast, had seen bloodshed, terror, death. He had suffered the violent death of his own father. He had contributed to the terror himself. He was marked. Yes, thought Kevin, there is a lot to remember, and to try to forgive. But he and Gerald had never been the easiest of friends and he knew that he would not be able to control himself indefinitely, no matter how much he remembered. He would give Gerald a month. A fair trial. After that, he would have to go. A trial? That didn't seem the right word to be using.

"This is our stop," said Kevin.

The smell of frying bacon met them as they opened the door making the saliva run in their mouths. Sadie stood by the cooker, the fish slice in her hand. The room was clean and tidy, the table set. Kevin's heart warmed towards her.

"Sadie love, this here is Gerald."

Sadie put down the fish slice and turned to them. She saw a boy who looked much as Kevin had done at seventeen, the same dark thick hair, brown eyes, strong, well-built body, but the expression on the face was different, much harder, and the mouth was set in a line, stubborn and a little twisted. This boy seemed more than seventeen at first glance; it was only as she stared longer that she saw that he was still quite young, somewhere inside.

"Hello Gerald," she said.

"Hello." He spoke guardedly, his eyes narrowing. He had resented his brother marrying a Protestant, had called him a traitor for it. He did not look as if he had accepted it yet. Kevin wondered again why he had agreed to come at all.

"Sit down then," said Sadie. "Your breakfast is ready. Kevin, pour Gerald some tea, will you? There's a fresh pot on the table."

Breakfast was difficult. Gerald did not speak, except to answer yes or no when directly addressed. He offered no information about himself or his plans for the future. He ate everything set before him without a word of thanks or appreciation.

"I'll wash up, Sadie," said Kevin.

"O.K., thanks. I'll away out for my shopping before Brendan wakes."

She escaped thankfully, glad to leave the brothers behind.

Kevin filled the basin with hot water, squirted in some washing-up liquid. Gerald sat back and watched with a look of amusement on his face.

"That's a fine sight," he said, "me brother Kevin with his hands in the sink like a woman."

"And why not?" asked Kevin calmly.

"You'll never catch me doing woman's work. Our da never did."

"And look at our ma now!"

"What's the use in having a woman if she doesn't wash the dishes for you?"

"You're about twenty years behind the times, boy."

"Ah, it's only cissies that get nagged into doing the women's work for them."

"Indeed? I wouldn't advise you to class me as such." Kevin looked him squarely in the face. "It might be to your cost if you did. I've flattened you before, Gerald, and you'll find I'll do it again if I have to. And there's another thing: it's only those men who have no confidence in themselves that are afraid to be seen doing women's work."

Gerald subsided but his face was dark with temper. He

began to tap one foot on the floor keeping up a steady tattoo. Kevin dried the plates, put them away.

"Some joint this is," said Gerald.

"If you don't like it you don't have to stay. We're not fussy." After only a couple of hours Kevin felt his patience paper-thin already. It would take little for him to throw his brother out into the street and his bag after him. Was that what Gerald wanted? From the way he was going on, you would almost think so.

"You needn't think I wanted to come."

"Why did you then?"

"Not much choice, had I?"

"You're not going to tell me that our mother made you? She couldn't make you do anything you didn't want to do, could she now?"

"I'd no money."

"Great! So you have come to sponge off me. What about your pals? Couldn't they have helped you out?"

Gerald got up. "Think I'll go for a dander. I could do to stretch me legs."

Kevin shook his head. Of all his eight brothers and sisters this was the one he got on with least. He didn't know how he ticked inside. And he didn't trust him: this was the worst thing of all. He would have to watch him closely.

Gerald came back at lunch-time. Where had he been? asked Kevin. Walking, he said. He ate his lunch silently, hunched over the table. Would he like to go to the football? asked Kevin. He shrugged. He didn't mind, he supposed he might as well if there was nothing else going. Sadie opened her mouth, closed it again, swallowed. She rose quickly to clear the table.

Gerald stood sullenly on the terrace beside Kevin and Bill, showing no reaction to the game. He might as well have been staring at a blank wall. He spoiled Kevin's enjoyment, for all the time Kevin was conscious of his brother, of the dark sour face, the hunched shoulders and aggressive body. The boy was as tense as a coiled spring. Antagonism and resentment mounted in Kevin. Why should he put up with this?

Hadn't he enough on his plate as it was? On his other side Bill was roaring with the crowd, caught up in the game, his eyes alight in his open, honest face. Why should he inflict Gerald on Bill either?

His brother's keeper. It was a role he did not want. But he supposed it was one of those things you had to take at times whether you wanted it or not.

Liverpool scored. The crowd rose in an upsurge of delight, all except for Kevin and his brother.

"What about a drink?" said Bill as they were leaving the ground afterwards.

"See you," said Gerald. He veered off sharply and left them without another word.

"Are you coming then, Kevin?" said Bill.

"No, I'll need to go in case Gerald gets home before me. I can't leave Sadie to cope with him. What would you do with a brother like that, Bill?"

"Kick him," said Bill.

Kevin sighed. It wasn't as simple as that: a kick would solve nothing. Gerald was almost immune to violence; he had seen too much of it.

Kevin stopped off at Mrs Hignett's for a copy of the *Liverpool Echo*. When he got home he spread it on the table and studied the 'Situations Vacant'. He read them nightly, always hoping there might be something for himself, but now he was looking for two jobs. He would get Gerald to sign on at the Labour Exchange on Monday, but he thought there would be little chance of a job for the boy. Unemployment was high in the city, especially in Gerald's age group.

"Found anything?" Sadie leaned her chin on Kevin's shoulder, putting her arm round his neck.

"There's one here: delivery boy wanted. Can't see much else he would have a chance of." Kevin folded the paper.

"Where is he now?"

"Who knows?"

"He doesn't know anyone in Liverpool, does he? You don't think he'll get up to anything? Planting bombs or that?"

"Don't think so. I've been through his bag. Terrible thing

to have to do to your own brother, isn't it? But I couldn't take the risk. There wasn't a thing there but his clothes, not even a bit of paper or a letter."

It was their turn to have Bill and Kitty for the evening. Sadie cut sandwiches and baked an apple tart, Kevin went out and bought beer and lemonade.

"Still no sign of Gerald?" said Kevin.

"Maybe he'll stay out all evening," said Sadie hopefully.

But Gerald came in just after Kitty and Bill arrived. Sadie was in full flood telling Kitty how ghastly he was, what a moron, what an ill-mannered lump, when the door opened. In the silence that followed Sadie was heard to groan.

Gerald lay on the settee all evening, his arms behind his head, and chewed gum. But his dark eyes missed nothing; they flickered watchfully, never at peace.

"Big brother is watching you," said Sadie.

Kitty giggled, Kevin frowned.

"Well, I'm not a saint," said Sadie to Kevin. "And if you imagine I'm going to turn into one you've got another think coming!"

Kevin grinned. "I'd be an eejit if I expected that."

Sadie passed round the sandwiches.

"Are you wanting one?" she asked Gerald.

"Might as well." He reached out a hand and took two.

"Charming isn't he?" said Sadie as she turned back to Kitty.

On Monday morning Gerald took the clipping that Kevin had cut from the *Echo* and went out. He returned at lunch-time.

"Any luck?" asked Sadie.

"No."

"Labour Exchange?"

"Nothing doing there either."

She set a plate of sausages and beans in front of him. He cleared it quickly, asked if there was any more.

"Afraid not. We've enough trouble as it is feeding the three of us, you know. It'll be a real worry for Kevin if you don't find a job."

Gerald did not reply: he got up and left the house. Sadie went upstairs to Kitty's to let off steam.

"I won't be able to hold my tongue, Kitty. Before long I'll just let rip at him."

"I bet you will." Kitty laughed. "It might be the best thing for him."

They took their babies out for a walk. It was a crisp sunny afternoon. They went into Sefton Park and scuffed their feet through the fallen leaves.

"I used to like doing this when I was a kid," said Sadie. "Me too."

"You know, I still like doing most of the things I did then."

In the garden of one of the big houses looking over the park someone was lighting a bonfire.

"Come on," said Sadie, making for it.

They stood by the gate and watched the flames licking round the big pile of twigs and leaves and the thin spiral of smoke going straight up into the still air; and then, all of a sudden, the bonfire was fully alight, spitting and sizzling, crackling and roaring, brilliant with reds, oranges and yellows. The smell was sweet, thick and pungent. Sadie and Kitty drew in deep breaths.

"Nothing like a good fire," said the man leaning on the rake. The fire-maker himself.

"You're right there," said Sadie.

They watched till the fire had almost burned itself out. The man spread the last flickers of life across the ground, stamped on them with his heavy boots. The garden looked dull and dead now.

Sadie and Kitty pushed their prams out of the park as the day was dwindling and turning cold.

On the corner by Mrs Hignett's shop was a group of youths. One sat astride a motor bike, two squatted on the edge of the kerb, the others lounged against the wall. Nothing to do, nowhere to go. Boredom came from them in waves.

"Do them good to run round the park a few times," said Sadie.

"Isn't that Gerald with them?" said Kitty.

"Yes, it is. And Gabriel Paradise is there too."

"Gerald's got into good company quickly, hasn't he?" said Kitty drily.

"I'm thinking he has a natural bent that way."

The boys moved off before the girls reached the shop. Here Sadie and Kitty parted. Kitty went straight home, Sadie had to buy something for tea. She was in and out of the shop a dozen times a day, she had no method of shopping like Kitty who bought a load of groceries at once. That didn't suit Sadie.

"Ah, Sadie," said Mrs Hignett, "I was wanting a word with you."

She was serving another woman. Sadie waited, bothered a bit by the way Mrs Hignett had spoken.

The other woman put her money on the counter, lifted her basket and went out, pulling the door behind her.

"Is there something wrong, Mrs Hignett?" asked Sadie.

"Well...." Mrs Hignett shook her head. "Sadie, I don't like saying this but I think I've got to."

"Do I owe you any money or anything? I can't remember...."

"No, no, you're all paid up. More than I can say for some." Mrs Hignett pushed a box of liquorice sticks aside and leant on the counter. "No, it's that young brother of Kevin's."

Sadie moaned. "I might have known." She sat down on the upright chair on her side of the counter. "What's he done? Tell me the worst!"

"Well I can't be certain," said Mrs Hignett carefully, "but I'm as sure as I can be. I think he's been lifting stuff. He's been in and out a few times buying a bar of chocolate, chewing gum, things like that, and every time he comes in there seems to be something gone afterwards. I know I've things lying everywhere but I've got a pretty good idea what there is. I'm pretty sure he took some chocolate one time and a couple of packets of fags this afternoon. I usually keep the cigarettes behind me where they're safe but I'd laid out two packets on the counter when I was making up the order for old Mr Gavin. Then some customers came in and I had to leave the things lying. Your Gerald was in too. I saw him standing there eyeing them. I was watching him but devil the moment I took my eyes off him he must have whipped them for I didn't actually see him take them."

Sadie listened with a feeling of doom, knowing that Mrs Hignett was probably right. Gerald was not to be trusted and he had little money.

"Did you ask him?" she said.

"Oh, I asked him. 'Did you see those cigarettes on the counter?' I said to him, and there was not a flicker in his eyes. He stared back at me as calm as anything and said he had not. He's a cool customer that one!"

"I'm sorry, Mrs Hignett." Sadie opened her purse. "How much do I owe you?"

"Oh it's not for you—"

"Of course it is. He's living with us. He's our responsibility."

Responsibility! Sadie stormed at Kevin when he came home. Why should they be responsible for Gerald. They couldn't afford to be. Three days Gerald had been with them, and he was in trouble already.

"I couldn't afford to buy anything for the tea after I'd paid Mrs Hignett. You'll have to eat beans on toast."

"That's not the problem," said Kevin. "What I'm going to have for tea I mean. I don't care about that. But what am I going to do with Gerald?"

Gerald came in as they were finishing their meal. He sat down at the table.

"You're out of luck the night," said Sadie, starting to clear up. "I had to pay your debts at the shop. Or make good your thieving, that'd be nearer the truth, and I hadn't enough left for food."

"What are you talking about?"

"You know! Two packets of cigarettes for a start."

Gerald walked out.

"That's his answer to everything," said Sadie.

Kevin went after him, catching him at the end of the street.

"I want to talk to you, Gerald."

Gerald tried to shake his brother's hand from his arm but found he was held fast.

"You can't go on like this and live with us. Now I'm warning you, Gerald! If you want to go on living the way you're doing then you can find a room and keep yourself. It's up to you. But think of it. Think hard! For there'll be no one else around to help you."

Gerald said nothing. Kevin took his hand away and walked back home.

"I don't know how to get through to him," he said to Sadie. "Where to start even."

Sadie started on Gerald in the morning when he was lying in bed on the settee.

"You haven't half the guts your brother has," she informed him. "Heaven only knows how you came to be in the same family! Lying there in your bed bone idle. And a thief into the bargain. You're a disgrace to your family. And your country too. It's the likes of you that gives the rest of us a bad name."

He turned over to face the wall.

"You can't even talk to me, can you?"

"I can talk all right. But why should I want to talk to the likes of you?"

"To a Prod, d'you mean? Oh, you might not want to talk to me but you'll live off me back, that's all! Oh, you'll do that all right."

There came a knock on the door, and Maria entered.

"Maria, you off school again the day?" said Sadie disapprovingly, forgetting that she herself had never passed up an opportunity to have a day off school. "Come and see this lazy good-for-nothing jerk of a brother-in-law that I have. Look, Maria, look at that! Did you ever see the likes of it in all your born days?"

"Sadie," said Maria softly, pleading with her not to be so harsh. She stood just inside the room, looking embarrassed.

"I'll take Maria into the bedroom," said Sadie to Gerald, "so that you can get your clothes on."

They went into the bedroom and hung over Brendan's cot admiringly. Five minutes later they returned to the kitchen to find Gerald sitting on the edge of the settee putting on his shoes. He kept his face bent down and did not look at them.

"I have to nip along to Mrs Hignett's for a minute," said Sadie. "Are you coming, Maria?"

"Shall I stay, in case Brendan wakes?"

Sadie was longer in the shop than she had intended—not an unusual occurrence—and when she came back past the window she heard voices and the rattle of cups. She came in to find Maria and Gerald sitting at opposite sides of the table.

"I made Gerald some tea and toast, Sadie," said Maria. "Was that all right? He said he was starving."

"He'd good reason to be starving," said Sadie meaningfully. Gerald looked up at her quickly, his eyes asking her not to say why. She did not.

She sat down at the table with them and took a cup of tea. She glanced sideways at Gerald. So he cared about something, did he? At least it was a start if he wanted to keep his pride in front of a girl.

"We have a lot of trouble at home this morning," said Maria sadly. "That's why mother kept me from school. Gabriel has been arrested."

Sadie eyed Gerald sharply and then said to Maria, "What's he done?"

"He broke into an off-licence late last night with some other boys. We knew something like this was going to happen. But what could we do?" Maria's voice wavered, then steadied. "I must go. Mother will need me."

When she had gone, Gerald said, "I wasn't with them."

"I hope not."

"I wasn't." He looked Sadie in the eye.

"O.K., I believe you." She sighed. "Gerald," she said quietly, "you'll end up like that if you're not careful."

He shrugged.

"Can't you do anything but shrug?" she cried with exasperation.

He was away for the rest of the day.

"What can he be doing all this time?" Sadie said to Kevin.

"I haven't set eyes on him since morning."

"Walking the streets, I suppose. What else? He's no money to speak of. He's different, Sadie, from what he was at home. He was fierier then, full of bravado, taking on the world. Now he's still full of aggro, I'll grant you that, but he's quiet with it."

"Sullen."

"All right, sullen."

"He's no charmer certainly," said Sadie, making Kevin laugh. "Though Maria doesn't seem to mind him. But then she doesn't mind anybody. She's a saint."

Gerald came in very late, just as they were thinking of going to bed. Sadie offered him food but he'd eaten, he said. Fish and chips. A boy had bought them for him.

And he'd got himself a job: porter at the fruit market. He was to start the next day.

Chapter Seven

GERALD HAD to get up at four to be at the market for five. They did not hear him go. It was a relief to come into the kitchen in the morning and find it empty. Sadie sang as she cooked breakfast.

"Maybe he'll get himself a place to live now he's got his own wages," she said. "I'll ask around and see if anyone's got a room."

She found a widow who lived two streets away, a Mrs Jenkins, who had a room to let. It was not a bad room, certainly no worse than their bedroom, and cheap.

"He's a quiet boy," she told Mrs Jenkins. "Doesn't make a racket, play a record player or anything like that."

"As long as he's quiet and doesn't keep late hours. I'd give him his evening meal."

Sadie drank a cup of tea with Mrs Jenkins. Mr Jenkins had been a seaman, away as much as he'd been at home, and last year, just before he was due to retire, he'd gone and got himself knocked down by a car and killed. He'd been drinking of course. He'd always been a heavy drinker. A man who drank was a cross for any woman. Mrs Jenkins hoped Sadie's husband didn't drink? Oh no, said Sadie, he didn't like the stuff at all. It was just as well or she'd rue the day she married, declared Mrs Jenkins. She was young to be married, wasn't she? She'd be far better enjoying herself while she could. Mrs Jenkins' mournful voice went on and on. Sadie thought it wasn't surprising Mr Jenkins had been a heavy drinker. She escaped as soon as she could after promising to send Gerald round in the evening.

He came home in the early afternoon; he was dirty and tired. Job was O.K., he said, nothing more. She left it until tea-time to tell him about Mrs Jenkins' room. He was quiet after she told him.

"It's nice and clean and she'll cook you a hot meal every night. Cheap too, as things go these days."

"Will you go and look at it, Gerald?" asked Kevin.

"I suppose so," said Gerald. "But I'd rather stay here. I can pay for my keep now."

"But we haven't a room for you," said Sadie.

"I don't mind the settee."

Kevin looked at Sadie. She stared blankly back at him.

"Well, I don't know, Gerald," said Kevin.

"Just for a bit. A week or two."

They agreed: just for a week or two. Though why he wanted to stay at all was beyond Sadie.

"You'd think he'd be pleased to get away from us," she said to Maria who came to keep her company whilst Kevin was out at a darts match.

"Maybe he would be lonely," suggested Maria. "Maybe he wants to be part of the family."

"But we're always narking at him and he hardly cracks his face with a smile when he comes in. He's as sour as week-old milk."

"Perhaps he wants to smile, but can't. He has nice eyes. Yes, I think so. There is a lot of pain at the back of them!"

"Don't tell me you fancy him, Maria!"

Maria laughed. "No. But I'm sorry for him."

"You'd be sorry for Jack the Ripper. You're so good, Maria," said Sadie seriously. "Now take me! I'm full of all sorts of bad things. My mother used to say I'd the devil inside me."

"But you have good things too, Sadie. And I am not all good, or patient. Oh no!" Maria laughed again, then sobered.

"Not with Gabriel anyway, not with him."

Gerald came home before Kevin that evening. His face was grey with fatigue. The early start and the hard work of lifting and carrying had taken their toll. He collapsed on to the settee and let his head flop back against the wall.

"Would you like a cup of cocoa?" asked Sadie. "I was just going to make one for Maria."

"Thanks." His eyelids were flickering, scarcely able to stay open. And by the time he had finished they were giving up the struggle and settling on his cheeks. Sadie lifted his cup from the settee and put it on the table.

"He looks more like Kevin when he's sleeping," she said.

"That should make you like him better then," said Maria softly.

Soon a pattern was established: Gerald went out to work whilst they slept, returned in the early afternoon, ate, went out, returned at tea-time, ate, went out again. When he did stay in he read sport and racing papers—he was mad keen on horses—or lay on the settee with his eyes shut. He found the work at the market hard, he told Kevin, but he wasn't complaining. He told them very little at all about anything.

"He drives me mad," said Sadie. "He's so *silent*."

"Doesn't suit you that, does it?" said Kevin.

"I like people to talk to me."

"And if he was in too much you'd be grousing!"

"He's in too much as it is, just being with us every meal time, knowing he's sleeping through the wall every night. Kevin, it's near on two weeks now since he asked if he could stay. Don't you think it's about time he was going round to take a look at Mrs Jenkins' room?"

"I'll ask him tonight," Kevin promised.

Gerald came in then and they sat down to eat. Sadie was in the middle of pouring tea when there was an enormous bang outside. They felt the ground move. Sadie dropped the teapot, splashing her feet with hot tea.

"It's a bomb," cried Gerald, leaping to his feet.

"Don't be daft," said Kevin. "It can't be."

"It is, it is!"

They ran out of the room into the street. One of the houses across the road was sagging in the middle.

"You see!" shouted Gerald. He was gesticulating wildly, throwing his arms around. "I told you, I told you! Don't you think I don't know what the sound of a bomb going off is like? *Well, don't you?*" He was almost screaming.

"It's all right, Gerald. Of course you know." Kevin spoke soothingly, as he might to Brendan. His younger brother looked half crazed about the eyes: he seemed to see beyond the house across the street. "Away and sit down, lad."

Sadie came up behind them carrying Brendan in her arms. He had been the first thing she thought of when the room rocked. Her heart was still thumping madly.

People were running up and down the street, doors and windows were opening; Kevin crossed the road. Gerald stayed where he was, in the doorway, leaning against the jamb. The wildness had gone from him now, and he was trembling.

"Maybe you should go and help too, Gerald," said Sadie, and then she saw that he could not move. He was staring across the street like one hypnotised. "Are you all right?" she asked but he did not seem to hear her. She put her hand on his arm and tugged him backwards into the room. "Come and sit down."

Docilely he allowed her to lead him to the settee. He sat on it staring in front of him with a glazed expression which frightened her. She left him, still carrying the baby, and went across the street after Kevin. He and another neighbour were carrying out the old woman who had lived in the ruined house. She was alive; she was moaning, clutching her head. Blood ran down her temple.

"Stay back, Sadie," said Kevin. "We think a gas main's burst. Someone's gone for the police and ambulance."

Sadie stayed back, because of Brendan. She went a little way along the street carrying him against her shoulder. She met Maria.

"Gerald's gone all funny, Maria. Come with me and see if you can help me do something for him."

Gerald still sat where she had put him down, looking as if he had not moved. His eyes were fixed on a spot on the wall.

"Gerald!" said Sadie. She snapped her fingers in front of him.

"Eh?" His eyes flickered a little.

"Are you cold?"

He was shivering violently. Sadie touched his hands and found they were like ice. Maria built up the fire, put a rug round his shoulders; Sadie poured a cup of tea from the pot and put it to his lips.

"He must be suffering from shock," said Maria. "Here, give me the cup. Brendan is wanting you."

She held the cup, gently, coaxing Gerald to drink. She wanted to be a nurse when she left school and Sadie could see in the way she tended Gerald that she would be exactly right for it.

Gradually Gerald loosened a little, his eyes began to blink and his hands warmed from the heat of the fire.

Sadie went to the window and watched the police and ambulance arriving. The old woman was taken away on a stretcher. The police were talking to Kevin and other people, asking questions, making notes in their little books. And then a Gas Board van drove up.

"Looks like it was a gas main after all," she said. "Couldn't have been anything else really."

"A bomb," muttered Gerald.

"No," said Maria, "it wasn't a bomb."

"Yes, a bomb. I know it was a bomb," he cried out loudly again. "It killed him."

He closed his eyes and lay back. Maria joined Sadie by the window.

"Who does he mean? Who was killed?"

"His father was killed by a bomb. But that was nearly a couple of years back. You'd think he'd have got over that by this time."

"How do we know? Do you get over things like that so quickly?"

"You try to talk to him, Maria. He might speak to you.

He'll tell me nothing. I'll go out for a while."

Sadie took Brendan out and stood on the pavement. The street was full of kids trying to get nearer the house. The police were chasing them away and evacuating the houses on either side of the damaged one.

Kevin came to Sadie, his face streaked with dirt.

"How's Mrs Flanagan?"

"Think she'll be all right. She was lucky. It was some blast! Let's go inside, there's nothing else to be done and it's getting chilly for the wee fellow out here."

"I think we should go up to Kitty and Bill's. I want Maria to have a chance to talk to Gerald." And Sadie told Kevin about his brother.

Kitty made coffee and they stayed for an hour. When they got back downstairs they found Maria and Gerald sitting side by side on the settee. The crazed look had gone from Gerald's eyes: he looked limp and exhausted.

"Sorry about that," he mumbled. "Don't know what came over me. Had a kind of black-out."

"Not to worry," said Kevin. "As long as you're O.K. now?"

Gerald nodded.

"I'm needing one or two things at the shop," said Sadie. "Will you chum me, Maria?"

She and Maria walked slowly along the street.

"Well, did he talk?"

"He did, yes." Maria shivered. "It's not a nice story."

Sadie linked her arm through the girl's. "Tell me, Maria."

"He and a friend—his best friend he said—were going to take a car and go for a joy-ride."

"I told you he was a wild one, didn't I?"

"They got the car door open and his friend got into the driving seat." Maria paused. "And then the car blew up. There was a bomb planted in it. Gerald was blown across the street, he was lucky. His friend was blown to bits. Gerald saw it happen right in front of his eyes!"

"How horrible!" Sadie cried out.

They continued to walk, arm in arm, quiet now. Sadie sighed.

"There is another possibility, Maria, I'm afraid."

"Yes?"

"Gerald and his friend might have been planting the bomb." Maria's large eyes widened, and Sadie nodded. "Yes, they might."

"But on the other hand they might not. I think we have to give him the benefit of the doubt, as they say, don't you?"

"Yes, I think we do. For whatever way it was it's obvious it's really shaken him up." They came to a standstill outside the shop. "I see now why he wanted out of Ireland," said Sadie.

Gerald was jumpy for several days; his hands were unsteady and he started at loud noises, a door slamming, car back-firing in the street. He would not look at the crumpled house across the street. Mrs Flanagan was making a successful recovery and those who had been evacuated were allowed to return home.

"We can't turn Gerald out now," said Kevin.

Sadie agreed, with a sigh. She had more sympathy for Gerald now, well of course she did, but she did not want him living with them indefinitely, and there was no sign that he would ever offer to move out of his own accord.

He went out less often now, spent long hours lying on the settee reading magazines and listening to the radio. When Maria came in he sat up and stopped yawning. It drove Sadie wild when he lay on the settee, dozed and yawned, and came to life only to eat, or talk to Maria.

"If only he weren't so lazy," she said to Kevin. "He never thinks to lift a hand to anything. He gets up from the table and leaves his dirty dishes lying as if I was his servant. And he drops his dirty overalls on the floor for me to pick up. I can tell well enough how he was brought up! But you grew up the same and you're not like that now."

"He's only seventeen."

"And I'm only nineteen. Though sometimes I feel more like ninety."

"You don't look it. Fifteen I'd say, if I saw you in the street."

"Thanks very much!" Sadie tossed her head. "I'm not wanting to look that either. But I don't know what's happened to that slinky sophisticated look I was dead bent on cultivating. I've always wanted to look mysterious. And what are you grinning about?"

"I was just thinking how pretty you look. Prettier even than when we first got married."

"Flattery'll get you nowhere. Sure you've a sweet tongue on you, Kevin McCoy. More than your brother has!"

The next day she had even more to complain of concerning Gerald for he got into a fight at work and was sacked. One of the men had been annoying him since he first went to work there, calling him names, Mick and Paddy and others, and saying that the whole of Ireland should be blown to bits and then the rest of the world would get some peace. Gerald's temper had been building up and up, until at last, with one more jibe, it erupted. He broke the other man's nose, and he himself came home with a black eye, a few bruises and his books.

"That was a brave bit of work you did the day." Kevin shook his head.

"He was asking for it."

"All right! Maybe he was. But you can see you get nowhere fighting. All you get is a sore face and lose your job."

"Sometimes you have to fight."

"And your shirt's ripped to bits," moaned Sadie.

"Sure what's a shirt?" said Gerald contemptuously.

"What indeed?" said Sadie. "It's something to cover your back with. And where are you to get another? From your brother Kevin I suppose?"

"I can get my own shirts. And I'll get a place to live on my own too. You're not wanting me here and I'm not staying where I'm not wanted." Gerald got up.

"Ach sit down!" Kevin pushed him back gently. "You're not fit to go anywhere on your own. But we'll have to do something. We can't go on as we are."

"You're right there," said Sadie. "But what have you in mind? You ought to start doing the football pools. My da does them every week."

Maria arrived. She popped in most evenings. That was for Gerald's benefit, Sadie told him, but he didn't know whether to believe her or not for Sadie was full of wild talk at times. He wasn't bothered whether Maria came or not, he told Sadie, and she said he should tell that to the Marines. Kevin often wished they would shut up for he could hardly get a minute's peace in the evenings to concentrate on the radios and televisions he was dismantling and reassembling. Gerald talked a lot more now, and he and Sadie argued—it came naturally to both of them—on all sorts of obvious topics like politics, Ireland, religion. When Kitty heard them at it she said she didn't know how they could be bothered. Fancy arguing about politics and religion!

Sadie recounted the tale of Gerald's fight to Maria now, dramatising it, colouring it a little more. "Isn't he the stupid nut, Maria? What would you do with him?"

Maria smiled at him and said she was sorry. "You must be feeling bad." She lifted his shirt and mended it, sewing it neatly and carefully. It took her most of the evening.

In the morning, Sadie had a headache. She snapped at Gerald and put off the television which he had just switched on.

"Surely you can live without the thing for ten minutes!"

Kitty looked in to say they'd clinched the deal on the house they'd been trying to buy in Manchester. Wasn't that great? Great, said Sadie. And they were to get immediate entry. It was a semi-detached house on an estate in a suburb, three bedrooms, through lounge-dining room, gas-fired central heating, garage, lovely garden, five years old, and had only been lived in by one young couple who had painted it up very nicely and were ever so nice themselves. Great, said Sadie. Kitty's voice grated through her head.

Sadie was glad when Kitty left.

Mrs Paradise looked in to say the social service people had been in half the morning poking their noses into everything, keeping Mr Paradise off his sleep. The social service didn't seem to think Gabriel's home was much good for him. Crystal had cried the whole time and Donna had been stroppy, but Mrs Paradise couldn't help that, could she now? But maybe it would be better for Gabriel if he had to go away for a bit, said Mrs Paradise. It would certainly be better for her.

Sadie was glad when Mrs Paradise left. She took two aspirins and felt a little better.

Outside it was raining, the kind of rain that would stay till nightfall, and they had to have the lights on in the kitchen. Brendan lay on a rug on the floor kicking his feet in the air and cooing.

"Isn't he well on for his age?" said Sadie. "Look at him, look how strong he is! Don't you think he is, Gerald?"

"Dunno."

"I'd have thought with all those babies your mother had that you'd have known all about them."

"Never paid much attention to them."

"You never pay much attention to anything if you ask me!"

"I didn't ask you."

Gerald lolled on the settee with the back of his head against the wall. He began to whistle through his teeth.

"Do you have to make that noise?"

"No." He stopped.

"Why don't you go to the pictures after lunch?"

"No money."

"Well neither have I so you needn't look at me."

"I wasn't looking at you, was I?"

"All right, keep your hair on! I'll make us a cup of tea."

She was getting just like her mother, thought Sadie, as she wielded the teapot. Her ma was never done drinking fly cups. Every time a neighbour opened the front door and called out, "Are you in, Aggie?" her mother would reach for the steaming kettle. Sadie used to say if you tapped her mother's veins you'd get tea out instead of blood.

They drank the tea. A little later Sadie did not feel so good again. She turned green and was sick, reaching the sink just in time.

"Are you all right, Sadie?" Gerald got to his feet for almost the first time that day.

"No," she groaned. "I feel as if I'm going to die."

He scratched his head. She got up and staggered into the bedroom where she flopped down on to the bed.

"Will I get a doctor?" Gerald called after her.

"Just fetch the basin from under the sink."

Gerald brought the basin; Sadie was sick again. Brendan began to roar at being abandoned on the kitchen floor. Gerald stood beside the bed gaping at Sadie.

"Dear, but you're a useless lump!"

"What'll I do?"

"Go and see to the baby for goodness sake! Can't you hear him screaming?" She retched again.

Gerald grabbed his nephew who seemed soft and floppy and to be spread in every direction. He laid him on the settee to straighten his clothes which were all twisted and rumpled. "What a twist you're in, boy!" Gerald shook his head. Brendan complained lustily throughout, kicking and resisting with all his might. "You're a real McCoy," his uncle told him. "Never done fighting back." He released the fingers of one small hand which had got stuck in the lacy holes of his cardigan newly knitted by Sadie's mother and received in the post that day.

"Now be quiet," said Gerald fiercely. "Your ma's not well."

Brendan's eyes widened, in surprise almost, and miraculously, he stopped crying. Gerald could not but help feeling a bit pleased with himself. "That's better," he said. It was easy enough with a baby: you just had to be firm.

He went back to the doorway of the bedroom. Sadie was lying with her eyes closed.

"Are you feeling any better?"

"A bit," she said weakly, opening her eyes with an effort. "Sure I think someone must have tapped me on the head. Could you give Brendan his bottle, do you think? There's one made up beside the sink. You just have to warm it."

Gerald closed the bedroom door. Brendan was still quiet;

he lay on the settee watching Gerald as he put the bottle in a jug of hot water, took a bib from the drying stand and lifted the baby. Gerald closed the curtains a bit more for people were often in the habit of glancing in as they passed, then he sat down in the armchair by the fire. He put the bib round the baby's neck, tied it carefully at the back. Brendan seized his finger and began to chew on it hopefully.

"Not that, you silly eejit!" Gerald tried the milk on the back of his hand the way he'd seen Sadie do. He'd sat so many afternoons watching her feed the child that he knew every move she made. It felt all right, as far as he could tell, and when he stuck the teat in the baby's mouth, Brendan seemed to think so too. He galloped through the milk like someone who had just emerged from the desert. He drained the bottle in record time; Gerald sat him up and a dollop of wind flew out of his milky mouth.

"Brilliant!" declared his uncle.

And then he changed his nappy. It took Sadie longer to get over the shock of that than her stomach upset.

"I don't know what you're making all the fuss about," said Gerald. "Sure there's nothing in it. Women are always making mountains out of molehills."

Chapter Eight

KITTY AND Bill had a farewell party and moved away to
Manchester. Sadie sat about mournfully for a day or two
missing Kitty badly, then she went upstairs and called on the
girl who had taken over the flat. Her name was Pat and she
had two small children who clung to her skirts and whined.
Pat herself was rather pale and wan but she was keen to be
friendly and she and Sadie walked in the park together with
their children.

"She's not bad I suppose," said Sadie to Kevin. "But it's
not the same as being with Kitty." But that was how things
were, Sadie knew that well enough from experience, and you
had to be prepared to move on all the time, to try something
else.

To move on was what they needed to do: Kevin was well
aware of that. He walked the streets thinking about it,
pondering on what could be done. They must make a drastic
change in their lives, for to go on as they were would send
them all screaming at one another's throats in the end. Sadie
and Gerald were tolerating one another now, got on well
enough at times, far better than Kevin had ever dared to
hope, but they were both explosive, given the right circumstances, which they often were. Gerald could get no work, was
at home on the settee half the day annoying Sadie and sharpen-

ing her tongue, and winter was well on its way, promising colder and wetter weather to keep them confined in the tight, damp kitchen. But what to do? Kevin leant on the rail at the pier and watched the gulls swooping overhead thinking it must be fine to be so free, and life to be so straightforward. To get another job would not be easy for him, and labouring at least paid a decent wage which he needed to keep his wife, son, brother, and mother too, partly. Yes, it must be fine to be a seagull.

Sadie got a letter from Kitty. Everything was super, including the neighbours who were terribly friendly and had asked her in for coffee to meet some of the other girls on the estate. Kitty hoped Sadie and Kevin would come soon to visit them; she was dying to show them the house.

"Let's go on Saturday," said Sadie.

"O.K.," said Kevin without enthusiasm, wondering what effect it would have on Sadie to see this marvellous house on this clean tidy suburban estate full of such nice friendly well-behaved people.

They took the train to Manchester and Bill met them at the station in his car.

"Well, well!" said Kevin, walking round it.

"It's not new, of course, but it's in good enough shape. Running a wee bit roughly."

"I'll take a look at it for you, if you like."

Sadie laughed. "I can see from the look in his eyes, Bill, that he can hardly wait to get his hands on it."

Bill drove them out to the estate on the edge of the city. Kitty, who had been waiting eagerly at the lounge window, came running out to meet them.

"It's marvellous to see you," she cried.

Even before they took off their coats she conducted Sadie round the house. "I'll let Bill show Kevin."

But Kevin already had his jacket off and the bonnet of the car up.

They went from room to room, Kitty pointing things out, Sadie admiring. The paint was fresh and bright and Kitty had worked hard sewing colourful curtains. "We need some more carpets and furniture, of course, but we'll get it all gradually. I'm saving for a bedroom suite. I've got a wee job three mornings a week, my mum keeps David for me, so it's all working out nicely."

The bathroom was all spruce and modern of course, so was the kitchen. Stainless steel sink, fitted cupboards, new white cooker.

"It's beautiful," said Sadie. "Like a little palace." It might have been her mother speaking in her! Her mother would certainly approve of Sadie living in a place like this, but Sadie could not begin to see how that day would ever come.

Sadie and Kitty sat in the through lounge-dining room and watched their husbands working on the car outside. They could see across the road into the house opposite too where a woman was feeding a baby, and if they looked out of the back window they could see a man reading a newspaper in his vest in the house behind. Sadie, who had been reared in the closed privacy of a small-windowed terraced house, felt as if she was sitting in a goldfish bowl. She kept looking over her shoulder. But Kitty seemed not to mind. She prattled on gaily about the neighbours. Nearly all the couples who lived on the estate were young, around her own age, and had small children.

"Don't know if I'd like that," said Sadie.

"Why not?" Kitty was astonished.

"I kind of like the mixture of ages. I'd miss people like Mrs Paradise and Mrs Hignett and Mr Fiske. Even old Mrs Francie."

"You're nuts," said Kitty good-naturedly.

"Likely." Sadie grinned.

After tea Kitty lit the lamps and drew the curtains, and Sadie liked the room better then.

"It's real cosy," she said. "Wish we could get a place of our own. A proper place."

"Hey, that reminds me!" Bill jumped up. He rummaged amongst a pile of newspapers. "I saw an ad that might interest you, Kevin."

"For a job?" asked Sadie.

"Yes." Bill found the paper, opened it up. "Now let me see. Yes, here it is. I marked it. See!" He gave the paper to Kevin.

Kevin read aloud, "Experienced farm worker wanted on large mixed farm in Cheshire. House provided—"

"A house?" shrieked Sadie.

"But I haven't any experience," said Kevin.

"You've had some," said Sadie. "In Tyrone."

"That was little enough."

"You can make it sound more," said Bill.

"And you're strong," said Sadie.

"You make me sound like a horse!" Kevin re-read the article, fingering his chin. "It's tempting though."

"Would you fancy the country?" said Kitty. "I couldn't take it myself. I like shops and people and things going on."

"I think I could take it," said Sadie, "if I'd a house of my own."

"I've had enough of the town," said Kevin. "It'd be just fine to have some fresh air and Brendan to have fields to play in when he gets bigger instead of kicking tin cans up the pavement."

"Are you going to go for it then?" asked Bill.

"There's no harm in giving it a try."

Bill fetched a pad of writing paper and they all helped to compose Kevin's letter. They did quite a bit of laughing and crumpling up of paper before they achieved something suitable.

"You have to build yourself up a bit," said Bill. "Blow your own trumpet. You won't get anywhere if you sound too modest."

"Make yourself sound desirable," said Kitty, rolling her eyes.

"He is desirable," said Sadie. "We'll enclose a photograph and they'll see for themselves. What about that one of you taken on the beach at Bangor? Where you're flexing your muscles and snarling because you were annoyed with me."

"You're a lot of use, you three!" Kevin chewed the end of the biro.

"Now, come on," said Bill, "there must be something good you can say about yourself."

"I am the greatest! That do?"

When Kevin read out the final letter it sounded rather flat and dull compared with all the suggestions that had been made.

"You sound very reliable," said Bill. "That's what they're looking for. They don't want any fly-by-night."

"Fat chance I'd have of flying by night, with a wife and baby and tearaway brother on my hands!" said Kevin gloomily, making them laugh. He licked the flap of the envelope, stuck it down, put on the stamp that Kitty held out. They went out to the post box on the corner, the four of them, and Kevin solemnly committed it to Her Majesty's mail. Sadie crossed her fingers tight, on both hands.

And then it was time for Bill to take them back to the station.

"It's been great, really great," said Sadie.

"Next time you must stay the night," said Kitty. "We should have another bed by then. And let's know the minute you hear anything about the job."

A week later Kevin received a letter asking him to come for an interview at the farm the following Saturday, and suggesting that he bring his wife with him.

The journey took about two hours altogether, travelling by train to Chester and then by bus to the farm. They left Brendan with Maria. Sadie grew more and more excited with every mile they covered and by the time they were on the bus she could hardly sit still.

"Look, Kevin, a canal! And boats. We could get a boat. Oh there's a lovely long boat."

"Boats cost a lot of money."

"So does living." Sadie kept her face pressed close to the window.

"I don't suppose I'll get as good money on the farm as labouring."

But Sadie was not listening. She was too preoccupied with

the countryside. The trees were bare and a fine mist hovered over the fields. Black and white cows grazed. Friesians. Kevin had checked on that, not wanting to be a complete fool when he talked with the farmer. "It pays to do your homework beforehand," Bill had said. It was lush country, fertile, and the farms well-kept. The richest county in England, Bill had told Kevin. The farmhouses were for the most part large, brick built, with good-sized barns, all in fine trim, with neatly clipped hedges and white painted fences. Horses too. Lots of horses. They passed a few children on ponies and Sadie wondered how Brendan would like riding.

"He's a bit small yet," said Kevin.

"It would be nice if we could get a pony for him."

"A boat. Now a pony. Is there anything else you'd fancy?"

"A wee car, like Bill and Kitty. Well, why not? A cheap one, Kevin. You're a marvel at making things go."

"I'd need to be a magician to conjure up all the things you fancy."

The bus stopped in a village two miles from the farm. The village consisted of a street of houses, some brick, some black and white half-timbered, a pub, a small shop that looked as if it would sell almost anything, and a primary school.

"There's a school for Brendan," said Sadie.

"You've moved in already, haven't you?" Kevin nodded at the street. "How do you fancy it then? That'd be your shopping centre."

"Well, it's not much like Liverpool, I'll grant you that. But if you got a car then we could run into Chester. It looked nice, from what we saw of it, all those black and white houses and the Roman wall going right round the middle. And it's lovely by the river too, so Mrs Fiske...." Sadie ran on, her mind bursting with plans.

The bus took on a few more passengers and started off again.

The road now was narrower, twisting and winding, with trees fringing either side. In spring they would make a tunnel of green. The trees gave way to a low white fence; beyond the fence smooth parkland rolled, fine large trees spreading their branches here and there. Elegant horses cropped the grass. Kevin could see at once they were well-bred by the slender grace of their legs, the way they moved, the rich deep colour of their coats. Set back in the park, screened by bushes and trees, they could make out a large stone house.

"That's Ellersley Hall," said the conductor.

It was much grander than they had imagined. Kevin had thought of it being a farm like the one his family lived on in Tyrone, a modest affair where the farmer worked on the soil himself and strode about in muddy boots. But it seemed unlikely that the owner of that large house would have muddy boots. It was more of an estate than an ordinary farm. "I'll let you off here then," said the conductor.

They got off the bus at the gatehouse lodge. The drive stretched away out of sight amongst rhododendron bushes.

"It's a bit posh," said Kevin hesitantly.

"Well what's up with that?" demanded Sadie. "You're good enough for anybody."

They knocked on the door of the lodge. No one answered so Sadie peered in at the windows.

"For dear sake, Sadie! Somebody might come."

"Nobody at home."

They set off up the drive. Water dripped from the bushes; the undergrowth was damp. A small breeze swirled up and blew some drops of water from a branch on to Sadie's face. She shivered and took Kevin's arm.

"Midwinter's not the best time to be seeing the place," he said.

At the end of the drive they stopped to survey the house in front of them. It was enormous, gabled and turreted, ivy-covered window after window staring blankly out at the fading afternoon.

"It's a bit much," said Kevin.

"Wouldn't say no to it. Not if I was offered it."

There was no movement around the house, no sounds except for the wind rustling the branches and the lonely cry of a bird.

"It's dead quiet isn't it?" Sadie had a sudden notion of

their street in Liverpool, with lights spilling from windows, kids yelling, people moving up and down, round and about. "Maybe I could say no to it after all. If I was offered something cosier."

"I don't really think you'll have the chance of saying yes or no. So come on, let's see if there's anyone at home here, now that we've come all this way."

They approached the stout oak door warily. It looked heavy and forbidding. Kevin rang the bell. They listened to its tinkle echoing away inside.

After a moment there were footsteps, then the door opened.

"Yes?" asked a stiffly polite man in dark clothes. A butler, Sadie supposed, though she had never set eyes on one in her life before, except in films. She smiled at him, thinking he could do to relax a bit.

"I have an appointment," said Kevin. "An interview for a job."

"What name?"

"McCoy. Kevin McCoy."

"One moment please."

He left the door slightly ajar but not open enough for Sadie to see anything other than a strip of shining tiled floor. They could smell the polish.

The door opened again. A tall elderly man in a tweed suit had taken the place of the butler.

"Can I help you?" he asked. He had a very smooth, pleasant voice.

Kevin launched into an explanation somewhat nervously.

"Ah, you want my farm manager, Mr Maxton. He lives in the house just down the road."

"Sorry to trouble you," said Kevin, furious with himself for not having realised that the owner of the estate would not be troubling himself with the hiring of farm staff.

"No trouble."

The man stepped outside, hands in pockets. "Chilly, isn't it? So you want to come and work for us do you?"

"I'd like to," said Kevin awkwardly.

The man walked down the drive with them asking them

about themselves, where they lived, how they felt about Ireland. Sadie chatted to him readily, telling him the story of their lives. Kevin answered more stiltedly.

"Kevin's young brother Gerald would come with us too," said Sadie. "He's mad keen on horses. I see you have quite a number out in the field there."

"I breed horses."

"You do? Well, maybe Gerald could give you a hand with them."

"Maybe he could," said the man with a smile.

At the lodge he stopped, faced down the road. "If you go down there for about a quarter of a mile you'll see Mr Maxton's house. All right?"

"Thanks very much," said Kevin.

"Thanks a lot," said Sadie. "See you again!"

"I hope so." The man smiled. "Good luck!"

He went back up the drive, they carried on down the road.

"Not a bad ould stick," said Sadie. "At first I thought he was going to be as stuffy as get out, but once he got going he was O.K."

"Once *you* get going!" Kevin shook his head. "He's probably a big racehorse fella and there you were offering him the services of our Gerald!"

"Well, why not? I'm not caring how big or wealthy he is. He's just another man."

"Aye, you're right, Sadie," Kevin squeezed her arm. "Dear but I don't know what I'd do without you!"

"You're not wanting to go flying at night then?"

"When I've got you?" He stopped and kissed her beside the wall. "There's your answer. And now for Mr Maxton."

Mr Maxton's house had smoke coming from the chimney and a light in the sitting room window. He turned out to be a small, square-shaped man of about sixty. His wife was large and smiled more than he did. He invited them into the chintz-covered sitting room, she disappeared into the kitchen to make them a cup of tea.

"You'll need a bit of warming up on this damp day," she said.

Sadie warmed her hands at the blazing log fire. Mr Maxton settled back in his chair, lit his pipe and began to question Kevin. He was too shrewd not to find out quickly that Kevin had little experience of farm matters.

"But I'm prepared to work hard," said Kevin. "I've worked hard all my life."

Sadie watched the blue and orange flames licking round the logs. Kevin had warned her to keep quiet. She would dearly have liked to tell Mr Maxton all about Kevin, what a good man he was, how solid and dependable, and how nice. Mr Maxton was not saying much, just asking questions, then puffing away whilst Kevin answered.

"There we are." Mrs Maxton brought in a tray laden with cups and saucers and plates of scones and cake. "All home baked," she said. "Fresh this morning."

Sadie tucked in; Kevin drank a cup of tea but said that he was not hungry. He told Mr Maxton about Gerald too.

"So there would be two of you." Mr Maxton nodded approvingly. He went on then to talk about wages, and when they had finished tea he asked if they would like to see the house.

It was another half mile or so down the road. The light was going fast now and they could only see the outline against the dark sky. It was brick and semi-detached, they could tell that, and there was a small garden at the front and a larger one round the back. Lights shone in the attached house. The head cowman and his wife lived there, said Mr Maxton.

"What was that?" Sadie ducked as something brushed close to her face.

"It's only a bat," said Mr Maxton.

"Only?"

He unlocked the door, switched on the lights and they went inside. Unfurnished and empty, with bare dusty floorboards, it looked bleak and not very friendly.

"It's really quite a nice little house," said Mr Maxton. "Sitting room at the front. Dining room-cum-living room at the back. And the kitchen off it." They mounted the stairs; he opened doors. "Bathroom. Bedroom. Another one. Good sized. And a little room, do for a child."

The rooms upstairs were low and coomb-ceilinged. So much space! It would be marvellous to have all these rooms, spread themselves out, have a room for Gerald and the little one for Brendan.

"It'd be very nice," said Kevin.

"You'd like it then?" Mr Martin turned to face him.

Kevin glanced at Sadie and she nodded. "Yes, we would indeed. If we could."

"Well, you've not much experience, but you're a healthy looking lad and I don't see why you shouldn't do well enough. I'm prepared to take a chance on you."

They went back to his house to discuss details. Sadie sat by the fire in a blissful warm dream in which she was putting up curtains in Brendan's room, painting the walls, pinning up pictures of animals.

They arranged to move in next Saturday, and Kevin and Gerald would start work the Monday following. Kevin and Mr Maxton shook hands on the deal.

"Goodbye," called Sadie and Kevin to Mr and Mrs Maxton who stood in their lighted doorway seeing them off.

"Goodbye," called the Maxtons.

The door closed, cutting off the light. They had to walk back to the village to get a bus. Only one came down past the farm twice daily. It was pitch black in the road. Sadie clung tightly to Kevin's arm. She felt more afraid of the country at night than she did of streets in the city. Branches crackled and shivered, strange unidentifiable noises came from the undergrowth. An owl hooted. At least, Kevin said it was an owl. She had never heard one before.

The night air was raw and damp. They turned up their collars and Sadie said that she would have to learn to knit properly so that she could make them all sweaters from the wool that looked like rope. She was wearing light shoes through which she felt every stone of the road and every patch of wetness. As they walked along by the white fence they caught sight of a glimmer of light from the big house. Mr Ellersley bred very fine horses, Mr Maxton had told Kevin;

he raced them too and had his own jockey.

The two miles to the village seemed a long way in the dark. From time to time they passed a cottage, and once or twice a car swept past flooding them with its lights.

They arrived in the village to find they had to wait an hour for the next bus to Chester, so they went into the pub. A few men stood by the bar. A fire crackled in the hearth; copper pans hanging on the wall above it shone in the light of the flames. Sadie dived for the corner seat.

They had a drink and a sandwich.

"Do you know," said Sadie, "something has just occurred to me?"

"Lightning has struck, eh?"

"You could say that. Kevin, we have no furniture. Not a single stick! And we're moving in a week."

Chapter Nine

THEY HAD a busy week. As Sadie had said, they had no furniture of their own, for what there was in their two rooms
belonged to the landlord. Kevin had an emergency fund put
away in the Post Office. They decided that this was a suitable
emergency.

Brendan was left with either Mrs Paradise or Maria whilst
Sadie and Gerald went in pursuit of furniture. They scoured
second-hand shops all over the city, attended sales. Anything
they bought had to be very cheap, stuff that nobody else
wanted.

"It might not be as good as Kitty's three-piece suite," said
Sadie, regarding a settee they had just bought at an auction,
"but it'll have to do." She had paid a pound for it. It was
the first time she had ever bid and she felt thrilled when the
auctioneer knocked it down to her. "In fact, Gerald," she
went on, "when you think of it, it's a real bargain getting
a whole settee for a pound. Kitty's cost eighty, so she said."
The sofa had a chintz cover basically fawn-coloured, with
green and orange leaves and flowers. It was filthy but, as
Sadie said, that was a mere detail and a good wash at the
launderette would soon sort that out. There were holes on
the arms of it but, as Sadie said, they could soon be mended.
She lifted the cover to look at what was underneath and
dropped it hastily again.

Gerald stood scratching his head. "There's one thing worrying me. How do we get it home?"

They had not thought of that. They were not very good at thinking ahead, grumbled Sadie. There were a number of removal men around lifting other things that had been bought and carrying them into their vans. She chose an elderly man in grey overalls with the name of his firm written in red across the pocket and approached him. How much would it cost to take their settee? She would have to see the boss, he said, so she did and the boss said three pounds.

"Three pounds," gasped Sadie. "But it only cost one."

"Can't help that, miss. It's not worth my while taking it for less."

Sadie returned to Gerald who had spread himself out on the settee.

"It's not bad at all," he said, bouncing up and down on it. "A bit lumpy but not bad."

"You're going to have to get up and carry it!"

It seemed there was nothing else for it. They staggered out of the hall with the sofa and laid it on the pavement.

"You're carrying it all the wrong way," said Gerald. "Honest, girls are useless when it comes to lifting! You need to get a better grip on it and lift it higher."

"Hasn't it got castors on it?" Sadie lifted the bottom frill. "Sure it has. Well, three anyway. Couldn't we push it a bit?"

They pushed and pulled, and carried it when the pavement was too uneven or when they had to cross a road.

"Excuse me please. Excuse me." Sadie smiled sweetly at everybody hoping for someone with a kind heart and strong arms. And there were many who did give them a hand for a few yards.

"Liverpudlians are dead friendly," said Sadie. "Now if this were London!"

A policeman helped them over a large intersection whilst the light said CROSS for their progress was so slow that the light might have changed another couple of times before they would have made it to the other side.

"Thanks a lot," said Sadie.

"You've some job on there," said the constable. "Going far?"

"Couple of miles."

"Rather you than me." He shook his head and off he went.

"Pity he couldn't have lent us a Black Maria," said Sadie. "Wouldn't that be a gas, Gerald, coming home in a police wagon?"

"Better than going away in one at any rate."

Every now and then they dropped the settee and sat down to take a rest.

"It's fine and handy carrying your own seating with you," said Sadie, leaning back and crossing her legs. "You can take a rest when you feel like it then."

"You certainly feel like it when you've got to carry it!"

"Look, Gerald, look down there! See the river! There's a boat crossing, must be the ferry to Wallasey. Oh I wouldn't mind setting sail. The sight of the water always affects me that way."

Whenever they stopped, Sadie made sure they had a view to enjoy. Everyone who passed turned to look at them. Sadie did not mind; she smiled, replied to those who addressed them, had a long chat with an old man with a dog and another with two women who were coming back from the town with their shopping and were glad to sit on the settee and take a bit of a rest. Oh yes, they knew what it was like to be young and hard up all right, and they praised Sadie warmly for her enterprise. Gerald sat and looked the other way whilst Sadie did her chatting. She liked watching the people go by too: old, young, thin, fat, men, women, children, black, white.

"There's great variety isn't there, Gerald? It really turns me on seeing all those different people."

"You'll not see many of them at the farm."

"No." The thought sobered her, then she cheered. "But it'll be different. There'll be other things to see."

When they reached their own street there was no shortage of helpers. Swarms of yelling children grabbed the settee.

Sadie and Gerald relinquished their hold and guided them up to the door. The next problem was to get it inside. They tipped and tilted it, and finally made it. And then there was another problem that they had not thought of before. Where would they put it? The kitchen was crammed already.

"The bedroom," said Sadie.

More tilting sideways, manoeuvring round the doorway, and they got the settee into the room. There was just enough space to squeeze it in beside the bed.

"Sure it's only for a week," said Sadie, dusting her hands off down the side of her jeans. "I'm gasping for a cup of tea. My throat's like sandpaper."

Kevin came in whilst they were drinking the tea. He thought the settee looked not half bad, considering, and that Sadie and Gerald had been smart to get it *and* bring it home. Maybe they should go into business together, the two of them? It was an idea, agreed Sadie, fired by the prospect of bargaining, making a profit, getting rich. Maybe!

Kevin sniffed. "Funny smell coming from it, isn't there?"

"You're imagining things. I'm going to wash the cover anyway." When Kevin went out she had a good sniff at the settee herself. Well there might be a bit of an aroma hanging about it but a good airing would soon sort that out. What could you expect for a pound? She would put it out in the back garden of the cottage for a few hours.

Kevin wanted to know where she was going to store anything else she bought. He was more inclined than she to think ahead. "There's no more room in here."

"We can pile some things on top of the settee," said Sadie. "Not much though."

Whilst they thought about it Sadie made more tea. Carrying furniture was thirsty work. The dust of centuries must have been in that settee.

"Mrs Hignett's got a store at the back of the shop," said Sadie. "It's only half full. I wonder if she'd mind ..."

Sadie went along to the shop to buy one or two things for tea. She told Mrs Hignett the story of the settee, describing it in full detail—how they had carried it through the streets of Liverpool. Mrs Hignett was amused. "You're quite a girl, Sadie. It would take a lot to get you down." And then Sadie got on to her real problem and Mrs Hignett said, "Well, I've got this space at the back. You're welcome to it if it's any good."

"Mrs Hignett, you're marvellous!" cried Sadie.

"And just a minute," said Mrs Hignett. "I'm thinking that maybe Mr Fiske might have an old handcart he could lend you. Why don't you go and have a word with him?"

Mr Fiske had been in the plumbing business for a long time and had taken his tools through the street on a cart before he bought his van. There was just a chance he might have kept it for he was the kind of man who threw nothing away.

"Oh yes, I've got it. It's in the shed," he said. "I'll lend it to you, lass. I'm only too pleased to find a use for it." He brought the cart out of the shed. Sadie rather fancied pushing it through the streets.

"It's far nicer than a van," she said.

"I think so too. But it's kind of slow. And there's no time for being slow these days. Do you know, Sadie, the missus was saying this morning that she wanted rid of two old kitchen chairs? They're getting in her road. She bought two new ones last week. Hang on a minute till I go and see."

"You're welcome," said Mrs Fiske, handing out the chairs. They were old-fashioned wooden ones, a bit scuffed but as sound as the day Mrs Fiske had bought them thirty years before. Sadie decided she would paint them white. "I'll see if there's anything else I'm wanting rid of while you're here," said Mrs Fiske. She brought out a half-moon shaped fireside rug in curly brown wool, a pouffe, a pair of curtains and a three-tiered cake stand in brown mahogany.

"Might come in useful," said Mrs Fiske, nodding at the cake stand which looked as if it had never had a plate of cakes set on it in its life. "If you were having visitors or that."

"Fantastic!" declared Sadie. "Thanks very much. Both of you."

Mrs Hignett came to the door of the shop to have a look at the cart. "Just the thing isn't it? Glad I thought of it." She leaned her hip against the wall. She was a woman who liked to lean, on the counter, against the wall. She was seldom seen upright. "I think I've one or two things I could give you, Sadie. Hang on a minute."

Sadie hung on, supporting herself between the handles of the cart. Like a donkey! She wouldn't mind taking to the streets collecting stuff. Kevin had once worked in the junk trade and toured the streets of Belfast with a Mr Kelly, the father of a girl who had fancied him. Sadie grinned, remembering that. It seemed a lifetime away.

To the things on the cart Mrs Hignett added a small chest of drawers with a broken leg, another kitchen chair, a coffee table (with a burn in the middle of it where Mr Hignett, God rest his soul, had once put a hot pot down), and two pillows.

"If I come across anything else I'll let you have it."

"Thanks, Mrs Hignett. Thanks a lot."

"Are you wanting to put this stuff in the back room then?"

"Yes please. But first I want to show them to Kevin."

Sadie parked the cart on the pavement outside their house. She rapped on the window and cried, "Rags and bones! Any old rags?"

"Trust you!" said Kevin, when he saw the loaded cart. "You'd find water in the desert."

The neighbours had a good clear out of lumber that had been cluttering their rooms, all sorts of things they had never quite been able to bring themselves to throw away. Two fireside chairs, a lamp, a carpet threadbare in the middle but not at all bad round the edges, two more rugs, curtains, a bedspread, a doormat, two lightshades, a basket chair with painted gilt edges, a kitchen cupboard a bit chipped but with life in it yet.

"You're fairly coming on," said Mrs Hignett, who was enjoying as much as Sadie seeing the pile grow.

At the sales Sadie and Gerald bought a double and single bed, two wardrobes, a chest of drawers and a kitchen table. They were exhausted by the time they pushed those large items of furniture home, piece by piece, on the cart. Sadie had second thoughts about going into the junk business. "I'd end up with muscles like Mr Universe," she said.

They already had blankets and linen, pots and pans, crockery and cutlery. So now they had enough to set up house. And Mr Fiske had offered to take their things to the farm in his van. He reckoned he could do it in two trips.

"Everyone's been so kind," sighed Sadie.

"Ah well, what are neighbours for?" said Mrs Hignett.

"You've been marvellous."

Mrs Hignett's back room was so full that she had to climb over furniture to reach her boxes, but she did not mind. It had added a bit of spice to life, she said.

"You'll need to come and visit us, Mrs Hignett," said Sadie.

"Oh I will. Some Sunday afternoon." She sometimes closed the shop at lunchtime on Sundays.

"Promise!" said Sadie.

Mrs Hignett promised. She quite liked the country, once in a while anyway, though she couldn't actually remember when she was last in it. Sadie went up the street inviting everyone to visit them.

"I don't know how I can come, Sadie," said Mrs Paradise. "With all these kids and the bus fares costing so much!"

"But Maria will come, won't you, Maria?" pleaded Sadie.

Maria smiled sadly. "Yes, I will come. But I will miss you, Sadie. Very much."

"You can come for week-ends, Maria. Friday to Sunday. We've got heaps and heaps of room. Will you?"

Maria nodded.

Sadie, Kevin, Gerald and Maria did not go to bed at all on Friday night. They were packing and people were dropping in to wish them luck and bring presents for their new home. There was a wall mirror from Mrs Hignett, a plaque from Mrs Carter their neighbour on the right side, a picture from Mrs Fiske, a flower vase from the Paradises, a tray from someone else, a china dog for the mantelpiece. Even Mrs Francie came out of her room and gave them a cracked jug for putting flowers in.

"Everyone's so kind," wailed Sadie again.

Maria sat quietly in the corner packing. Gerald sat near her wrapping crockery on her instructions. They scarcely spoke to one another.

Sadie made endless cups of tea for the women, Kevin gave the men beer. At two o'clock in the morning they felt hungry so they had beans on toast and mugs of cocoa. Sadie did not feel a bit tired; she could not have slept if she had tried.

At seven, as dawn was beginning to break over the street, she went to the shop. Mrs Hignett opened early for the papers. The lights were on, the counter was stacked with the morning papers, Mrs Hignett was yawning. She still had her rollers in, with a blue chiffon scarf wound round them, and she was wearing her pink quilted dressing gown.

"Do you know, Mrs Hignett, I'll have two miles to go to the nearest shop?"

"Two miles? I hope it's going to suit you, Sadie," said Mrs Hignett doubtfully.

"I hope so too," said Sadie.

She took her milk and fresh rolls and went back along the street. The sky was streaked with pink and red above the roofs. It was the last time she would walk along the street, as an inhabitant anyway. Really, it wasn't such a bad old place, there were lots worse. Much worse. Places you could be lonely in. She had never felt lonely here, and that was something.

They were leaving in an hour. Her eyes felt hot. She brushed them with the back of her hand.

"Silly ould fool that you are, Sadie McCoy," she said to herself. "Sure you're not going to Australia. You can come back and see everybody when you want to."

Or so she imagined, to ease the pain of going. But it would never be quite the same again, she knew that.

Chapter Ten

IN *the bleak midwinter* ...

The words from the Christmas carol jingled through Sadie's head as she stood at the window of her cottage looking out on the world. Her world now for three whole days. She could not believe that it was not very much longer, for the street in Liverpool seemed far far away. Kevin and Gerald were at work; she was alone with Brendan. Sleet was falling, thick wet sleet that blurred the trees; as soon as it hit the ground it disappeared. It would not have been so bad if it were snow, for then she could have looked forward to seeing it lying on branches and hedges, and to running out to make footprints in the crisp whiteness when it stopped falling. The sky was the colour of lead.

Kevin and Gerald had come in for lunch and now they were gone till tea-time. Whilst they ate they had talked to one another of farm matters. It was a good farm apparently, well-stocked and well-run, and the only drawback was that Gerald had not taken to Mr Maxton, nor Mr Maxton to him. Kevin said that Gerald would have to be patient. Sadie knew that was what she would have to be too and patience was not much in her line. She made a face at the sleet and the heavy sky. The brothers had barely addressed a word to her, apart from asking if there was more gravy, things like that: they had been too intent on their own talk.

A good fire crackled in the hearth behind her. There had been coal and logs in the shed when they arrived. They would have to buy their own coal in future but there were plenty of logs in the barn for the taking. Mrs Maxton had brought in a cake to welcome them. They had shared it with Mr Fiske and Maria and they had enjoyed sitting round the fire eating it and warming their cold hands. Mr Fiske had said the smell of the logs took him back to when he was a boy. And then he had had to go, taking Maria with him.

"Come back soon," Sadie had urged Maria.

Sadie sighed. She supposed it would be sleeting or raining in Liverpool too and the street would be deserted but Mrs Hignett would be in her shop leaning on the counter saying to everyone who came in, "Terrible day, isn't it?" And Mrs Paradise would be in her hot stuffy kitchen with the smell of drying nappies round her ready to stop whatever she was doing and offer a cup of coffee. Sadie sighed again, then spoke to herself sharply. "Ah give over! You sound like an ould wumman puffing and sighing. You knew it wasn't Piccadilly Circus you were coming to."

She examined the room to see if there was anything she could do. They had set the place to rights over the week-end, working until they dropped. The house was beginning to look like a place where people lived. The furniture was a bit tattered and bashed here and there and they had some funny colour schemes by the time they put everything together but on the whole it looked all right. She had sprayed the settee with eau-de-cologne to dilute the smell.

She switched on the radio, took up her knitting and sat down by the fire. She was knitting a thick ribbed sweater for Kevin in scarlet wool. She had cast on the stitches and done one row and that had taken ages for she had to restart three times. She seized the needles with determination. Millions of girls knitted so there was no reason why she should not too: so her mother had said, many times. She had never wanted to learn before, had done it carelessly at school dropping stitches and not noticing until she was half a dozen rows further on and the whole thing was in a mess. Taking it back used to be the last straw. "Too much talking, Sadie Jackson!" the teacher would say, twitching her long thin nose over the tangle of Sadie's knitting. Well she wouldn't do much talking here, that was for sure!

After four rows she laid it aside. Her fingers hurt and her arms ached. Four rows wasn't bad; in fact, for her, it was really very good. She yawned, put another log on the fire. They did indeed give off a marvellous smell. When summer came they would gather logs of their own in the wood. When summer came! On a day like this it did not seem likely that it would ever come again. It was difficult to believe that the sun would shine, that you could get too hot sitting in it and have to retreat under a tree for shade.

She tiptoed upstairs to take a look at Brendan. It bothered her a bit having him so far away from her, so every few minutes she went up to see that he was all right. He slept soundly in his cot, his fists clenched in front of him. He had been awake most of the morning so he would probably sleep the rest of the afternoon. She was tempted for a second to lift him and take him downstairs, so that she would have company. But she might get more than she bargained for: a bout of crying and grizzling until she fed him again and laid him down. She stood at the foot of his cot for a few minutes watching him. "Dear but you've changed my life, wee fella!" she said softly. "It's just as well I think you're worth it."

It was almost dark now in the sitting room. The sleet, if anything, had got thicker. Sadie watched, hypnotised, unable to take her eyes off the soft drifting flecks of whiteness. It was as if they were washing through her mind taking all her thoughts with them. She felt closed in, surrounded, trapped. There was nothing to be seen of the world. Was the world still there?

She shook herself, went to the kitchen to make a pot of tea. *Polly put the kettle on!* It was always something to do. She warmed her hands round the flame whilst she waited for the kettle to boil, and gazed out through the window at the back garden. It looked just the same as it did at the front. When she had poured the water into the little brown teapot she kept for herself she carried it through to the warmth of the sitting room.

After she had drunk two cups of tea she drew her feet up beside her on the settee and let her head slide down on the cushion.

She awoke to find the room dark, the fire low, almost dead. The world on the other side of the window was black. Putting on the light she saw that it was four o'clock. The fire was easily resurrected with a bit of puff and another log. She must have slept for more than an hour. She rubbed her leg where it was cramped and yawned, stretching herself as far as she could.

The sleet seemed to have stopped: the window was dry. She went to the front door and opened it. A cold wind swirled in around her making her shiver and hug her shoulders. The trees were shivering too, and rustling, and sighing. Beyond the garden there was nothing to be seen. Not a light anywhere, except for the one spilling out from her doorway on to the path. She went down the path a little way to look at the house beside them but it was dark too. The head cowman and his wife were late middle-aged and had little to say. They liked to keep themselves to themselves, Mr Maxton had said.

Sadie went back inside and closed the door. Kevin and Gerald should be home in an hour. She would have to wait till then for the sound of a step and a voice.

Kevin and Gerald both fell asleep half way through the evening.

"It's the air," said Kevin, struggling up, red-faced and smudge-eyed, some time later. "I'm not used to it."

"You're a great pair," said Sadie, who had knitted another four rows of the red jersey.

Gerald went off to bed early, yawning.

"At least he can go to bed if he wants to," said Kevin. "He doesn't have to sleep where we're sitting. It's really grand having a whole house to ourselves. It's working out rightly isn't it, Sadie?"

"I suppose so," said Sadie.

Kevin was too tired to notice the gloom in her voice, which she knew she had put on deliberately to try to draw his attention to *her* plight. It was all right for him and Gerald: their lives were busy and interesting. And then honesty crept in and she admitted to herself that of course they were working, and hard at that, out in frightful weather, and given the chance they would probably rather have stayed by the fire and slept on the settee. She could choose, within limits, how to spend her day; they could not. "Want a cup of cocoa?" she said.

As she watched the milk heating in the pan she made herself a promise. Tomorrow would be different. No matter what the weather was doing, she was going to pack Brendan into his pram and venture into the village. There was a shop there and houses, and that meant people.

The shop was closed. She tried the handle of the door again, then peered through the glass into the dim interior. There was a deep freeze on the left, rows of tins and jars, a clean and tidy counter, not littered like Mrs Hignett's, vegetables in boxes on the other side. She looked at her watch. Two o'clock. It must be shut for lunch. Mrs Hignett never shut for lunch, she just went through to her back room and ate her dinner and if the bell rang she got up and served. Sadie had got out of the habit of thinking about shops closing.

It was warmer today so it was raining instead of sleeting. She stood back against the door of the shop where she got a little shelter, hoping that the shopkeeper might look out and take pity on her. Rain bounced off the hood and apron of the pram, pleasing Brendan who lay watching it wide-eyed.

There was not a speck of life moving in the street, except for the rain. Not that she blamed anyone for staying indoors on a day like this. But even the houses looked dead; not a curtain was twitching or a face peeking out to see who it was waiting outside the shop. A car swooshed through the street spraying water to right and left and was gone. When she had passed the school she had heard children's voices, and the lights had been on. So the village was not quite dead.

"Piccadilly Circus," she said aloud. She stuck her hands deeper into her pockets and hunched her shoulders up round her ears. She would have to buy a pair of Wellingtons: her feet were soaking.

Fifteen minutes later there was still nothing happening inside the shop. She twisted the door handle again rattling the door, making as much noise as she could, but she was no match for the rain. It was keeping up a tattoo as if its life depended on it. The gutters were beginning to overflow. A few yards further down the road was the pub. She would go and ask what time the shop opened. There was one car parked outside the pub. Sadie put the brake on the pram and went inside.

"The shop?" said the publican. "Oh, it doesn't open at all this afternoon. It's the half-day."

"The half-day?" wailed Sadie. "But I've walked two miles to get here in all this rain. Me feet are like sponges."

"Newcomer to the district are you?"

Sadie told him who they were and where they were living. Oh yes, of course, he knew Mr Ellersley's place, nice place it was too, and Mr Ellersley, he was a nice man as well, he came in sometimes on a Sunday morning for a pint. Sadie and the publican had a long chat. The publican was called Mr Hughes, he came from across the border, in Wales, originally, and he and his wife had kept the pub for ten years.

"We're still incomers too, you might say."

"It takes a long time to get in round here."

"Ah well, country folk are more cautious than city ones."

"Tell me something to cheer me up!"

Mr Hughes laughed. "But when they do take you in then they're good friends. Why don't you dry yourself by the fire before you set off again?"

"Thanks, I'd like to. Oh, I nearly forgot! I've left the baby outside. Can I bring him in?"

"Certainly."

She lifted Brendan out of the pram and carried him into the pub.

"Could I have a Coca-cola please and a cheese sandwich?" she asked Mr Hughes.

"Just you sit by the fire and I'll bring it to you."

He brought his wife at the same time and introduced her to Sadie.

"Pleased to meet you, Sadie." Mrs Hughes sat down on the armchair at the other side of the fire. She looked at Brendan. "What a lovely boy he is then!"

Brendan seemed to like the look of her too and when she put out her arms for him he went happily into them. She had a nice broad lap to sit on, beads round her neck to pull, and a smiling jolly face. Sadie dried out, ate and drank, and enjoyed the rest and the company.

When she got up to go Mr Hughes would not let her pay. It was on the house this time. Sadie thanked him and said she was sure they'd see her husband in for a pint before long. "You'll know him: he's tall, dark and handsome!" Mr and Mrs Hughes laughed.

The rain had slackened and the sun was making an effort to break through a cloud. Sadie set off gaily, singing to Brendan. School was over and children were spilling out of the doorway. The village had come alive.

"Look at all those children, Brendan. One of these days you'll be coming out of there."

Would he? That was five years away. Would they still be here? So far, they had been wandering around like nomads. Before she married Sadie had lived for seventeen years in the same house; since then, in just over two years, she had moved four times, not counting a trip over to Ireland in between. She did not know if they would still be here in five years' time and she did not mind that she did not know. It would have driven her mother wild to keep shuttling about. When she got married she had expected to get her house and stay in it for the rest of her days.

They turned off on to the narrower road that ran along the side of the estate. The rain started up again, with the wind behind it. Sadie walked as close to the hedge as she could.

Everything, fields, hedges, trees, cows, Sadie herself, were dripping with water.

She passed the lodge at the end of Mr Ellersley's drive, then half a mile more and she came to the Maxtons. Mrs Maxton was standing at her window and when she saw Sadie she came to the door and beckoned to her to come in.

"Would you like a cup of tea, dear? I was just going to have one myself."

The kettle was boiling. Sadie sat down and told Mrs Maxton about her trip to the village. "So I'll have to go all the way back for my messages in the morning."

"It's a pity you didn't know about the half-day. And the grocer's van was along while you were out. He comes on a Wednesday afternoon."

"Trust me!"

Mrs Maxton lent Sadie a loaf, a half pound of butter and gave her six fresh eggs. Sadie reached home just in time to make tea. She was going to have to organise herself, that was for sure. The days of popping out to Mrs Hignett's shop were over.

Chapter Eleven

IT WAS a dark cold morning. A thin slice of moon hung above the rooftop of Ellersley Hall. Kevin and Gerald crossed the farmyard to the barn where the cows were waiting to be milked. They were helping Bert Halliday, their next door neighbour, who had hurt his back and was only allowed to do a limited amount of work. They had slept in—Kevin had forgotten to wind up the alarm clock—and had had to start the day without even a cup of tea to warm their stomachs. After the milking they would go home and have something to eat.

A cat ran in front of them.

"It was one of the black ones," said Kevin. "We should get good luck the day."

"We could be doing with some," said Gerald.

Gerald hated milking, said it was women's work; he would have preferred some other job. But there was no ploughing or planting in the middle of winter, Kevin told him, so what did he expect? And Gerald disliked Bert Halliday who, he said, spoke to him as if he was a child. It was only the man's way, said Kevin, there was nothing personal in it, but Gerald scowled and said the man didn't like him.

Halliday was already in the barn sitting on an upturned bucket in the corner smoking his pipe.

"Cold morning," said Kevin.

"Seen worse. You're late."

"I know. Sorry. We slept in."

"Cows don't sleep in."

The cows were mooing, heavy with milk.

"Better get on with it then," said Halliday.

"It's all right for him sitting on his rear end giving out orders," muttered Gerald, as he and Kevin fetched the pails and began to set up the machines for milking.

"Watch it, Gerald! He'll hear you."

"And why should I care if he does?" said Gerald a little louder. "He's not our jailer. Though he seems to fancy he is."

Halliday sat with his eyebrows bunched together, watching every move the boys made. He shot up suddenly.

"Not like that, you fool!" He pushed Gerald aside. "Do you want to cut the cow in half?"

"Who do you think you're calling a fool?" demanded Gerald.

"You! Well, aren't you?" Bert Halliday put a hand to his back. His face was twisted with pain. He had moved too quickly.

"Nobody gets away with calling me a fool."

"Don't they? We'll see about that. I'll call you what I like."

" 'Deed you won't."

"Leave it, Gerald," said Kevin.

"What do you think you're going to do about it? Go on strike?"

Halliday laughed, though there was no mirth in his laughter. It was a hard, sour noise. "That'd be a joke eh? One week at the job and then strike. You'd be out on the road with your books."

"And who's going to be put me out? You? And who else?"

"I wouldn't lay a finger on you." Halliday hobbled back to his seat. "You Irish are all the same. Always looking for a fight."

"I think," said Kevin, straightening himself, heat coming into his face, "you could be mistaken about that."

"Oh I know your kind well enough." Halliday nodded. He struck a match and relit his pipe.

"What's all this eh?" asked Mr Maxton, who had come into the barn unheard.

"I've been getting a bit of lip from these two," said Halliday.

"I think you should stick to the truth, Mr Halliday," said Kevin. "I've given you no lip, as you call it, and well you know it. And you called Gerald a fool to start with."

"He was putting the thing on the wrong way round." Halliday turned to Maxton. "They were late too, both of them."

"Five minutes," said Kevin.

"I think you should all calm off and get on with the work," said Maxton. "You'll need to be patient, Bert, you can't expect them to be as expert as you. Can you spare a minute? I was wanting a word with you. Come on over to the house and have a cup of tea."

Halliday went off with the farm manager.

"It's all right for him," said Gerald, "away off for a cup of tea. It'd freeze the daylights out of you this morning."

"It's not so bad in here," said Kevin. "In fact, it's quite warm." The cows' bodies gave off heat. The milk flowed freely, filling the aluminium cans. "You'll have to learn to make allowances for people, Gerald. I expect old Halliday's worked hard in his time. Up at the crack of dawn every day of his life. Now he's got a bad back and he's irritable."

"I'm not sure that I fancy getting up at dawn every day of my life."

"I don't mind. I quite like it. It's nice being out when everything's fresh."

They finished the milking, loaded the churns on to the lorry. They had twenty minutes before they need set off for the depot: time to go quickly back to the house and eat.

Halliday returned, eyed the cans, counted them.

"Hope your Highness is satisfied," said Gerald, who was leaning against the barn wall with his arms folded.

"What did you have to say that for?" asked Kevin, when they were on their way back to the house for breakfast. Gerald would try the patience of a saint.

"He asks for it."

"He's out to get you. If you're smart you won't give him the chance."

Sadie had a panful of creamy scrambled eggs and masses of hot buttered toast waiting for them. "There you are now," she said, dishing it out. She had built a big fire in the grate. "That should warm you up."

Kevin and Gerald ate quickly.

"Some life this is," said Gerald. "I don't know if I can stand it."

"You'll have to," said Sadie.

"I don't if I don't want to."

" 'Deed you do. You can't eat grass. Or sleep in the fields. None of us can."

"How would you like to put up with ould Halliday calling you names and insulting you?"

"We all have to put up with something we don't like." Sadie slapped down the teapot. "Sure we're all trying to do our best here, make some kind of life. You've got to too. You're not such a cissy that you'll start talking about giving up!"

Gerald pulled on his jacket and went out scowling.

"He's in a lovely mood," said Sadie. "Dear help the girl that gets him!"

Kevin gave her a kiss. "See you later, love." He grinned. "You're good at laying into him. Just like Ma!"

"Gee, thanks!"

Gerald sat silently in the passenger seat whilst Kevin drove to the depot. The sun was up now, a thin winter sun without heat, but it was bright and it gleamed over the brown-black earth and bare trees, changing them, softening them. Kevin thought the countryside looked very fine this morning. Beautiful. That was the word that came into his head as he steered the truck round a bend and saw a dazzle of light flickering through a wood on their left. It was not a word he often used. He liked the country this way, clean and sparse. He sang under his breath. He was glad that he had left the building site behind, and the dirty streets.

They delivered the milk, drove home. There was fodder to be prepared for the animals.

They were forking hay in the barn when Mr Maxton came in.

"You'll have to watch your tongue, lad," he warned Gerald. "I know Bert Halliday's none too easy to get on with but he's head cowman and very experienced."

Gerald made no reply. Mr Maxton tightened his mouth. Kevin watched anxiously. But there were some things he could not help Gerald with: he must find his own level and he, Kevin, could not jump in every two minutes offering excuses, or answering for him like a mother for a child.

As Mr Maxton turned to go, Mr Ellersley drove into the yard in his Land Rover.

"Ah, Maxton, I've been looking for you." Mr Ellersley got out. He saw the brothers and said, "And how are you boys getting on? Settling in?"

"Yes, thank you," said Kevin.

"Your wife liking her new house?"

"Very much."

"Good. I'm glad. Well, Maxton ...'

The two men went off across the yard together.

"It's all right for some," said Gerald. "Your wife liking her new house?" he said, imitating Mr Ellersley's very English accent. "Good! I'm glad."

"You've no call to be taking it out on him. He's done nothing to you. He's given you a job, hasn't he?"

"And does that mean I have to get down and lick his boots?"

"It just means you could be civil. If that's possible!"

Kevin was short with Gerald for the rest of the day. No wonder his mother had said the boy was a cross for her to bear! He did not see Gerald after mid-afternoon. He wondered vaguely where he might be but was too weary himself by that time to bother very much. And there was a limit as to how far he could go in this business of being his brother's keeper.

Gerald did not come by tea-time. They ate without him and afterwards Kevin took a torch and went back to the farm buildings to see if there was any sign of him.

"You don't imagine he's run off, do you?" said Sadie. "Without any of his stuff?"

"He's that hot-headed I don't know what he might do," said Kevin.

He met Gerald on the path.

"Sorry I'm late."

"Where have you been?"

"The stables. Boys, he's got some grand beasts there!" Gerald blew on his hands to warm them. "There's a real beauty, a three-year-old chestnut. He's going to be racing him at the Cheltenham Gold Cup." Gerald rambled on about the horses all the way home. He'd got on rightly with Bobby, the jockey, too, and Mr Wright the trainer.

Each afternoon after that, when Gerald finished work, he disappeared.

"He's beginning to smell like a stable," said Sadie.

The days shortened, and Christmas came. They passed the day quietly, eating and watching television. Mr Ellersley had given each worker a fat turkey and a bottle of port. Sadie said wistfully that it would have been rather nice to go up to Liverpool but they could not afford it and she knew it, so she mentioned it no more. She hung all the cards from their friends on a string across the room.

Will try to come and visit you soon, said Maria on her card. But the fare would be a problem for her and Sadie could think of no way of getting her there without money. It was a pity Mr Fiske wouldn't fancy a wee run down but she could hardly write and suggest it, could she?

"No," said Kevin firmly.

Will come to see you one of these days when the weather is better, wrote Kitty and Bill on their card.

"There's been nothing the matter with the weather," said Sadie.

"You're never done complaining about it," said Kevin.

"But they have a car. I have to hike on my own two feet."

"People imagine the country's impossible in winter when they've never been used to it. Kitty and Bill are real city slickers. Could you see Kitty living two miles from the nearest village?"

"No, but then I never used to think you'd ever see me doing it either."

Mrs Hignett said nothing about coming on her card; she merely signed it: *Regards, P. Hignett.*

On Boxing Day Gerald hitch-hiked up to Liverpool.

"Lucky devil!" said Sadie. "Hey, Kev, why don't we? Well I mean there's nothing to stop us. I'm game."

Kevin glanced over at Brendan. "Forgetting something?"

Gerald stayed away overnight, returned next day with good wishes from all their old neighbours and a box of *Black Magic* from Mrs Hignett who had said to tell Sadie she really missed her popping in and out.

"And how was Maria?" asked Sadie.

"All right. Still saving for her guitar." Gerald shook his head. "She'll never make it, that family takes all her money."

"Families have a habit of doing that," said Kevin. Since coming to the farm on a lower wage he had had to cut the money to his mother to two pounds a week. Every time she wrote now she complained that she could scarcely manage, the cost of living had soared so high.

"Write and tell her it's high for us too," said Sadie.

"I have. But she just ignores anything she doesn't want to see these days."

Gerald had started to send her a pound a week too but she still wrote complaining to Kevin.

The year turned, and the days began to lengthen slowly. Kevin enjoyed the extra daylight at the back end of the afternoon, he liked to walk home when there was still light in the sky. The winter sunsets were often incredible, on crisp and clear days, with the sky streaked with vivid colours, pink, orange, lemon, turquoise, indigo, blue. He walked home one afternoon watching the sky, admiring the black branches of the trees against it, thinking he had never seen such fine sunsets in his life before, when suddenly, arriving at his house, he realised they had a visitor. There was a motor bike parked against the side wall.

Sadie was in the kitchen standing by the stove.

"Who's here?"

Sadie made a face. "Friend of Gerald's from Belfast. Boy by the name of Jimmy Doyle."

Kevin frowned. "Doyle? There was a family in our street called Doyle. I believe there was a Jimmy; yes there was, friend of Gerald's. Right tearaway."

"I could tell he was no saint just by the look of him," said Sadie.

"What's he wanting with Gerald?"

"Passing by, he said. On his road to London. Thought he'd look in and say hello."

Kevin found Jimmy Doyle sitting by the fire in the sitting room.

"Hello, Jimmy."

"Hi." Jimmy grunted, not bothering to look up properly. He had his feet spread right across the rug in front of the fire.

Kevin stepped over his legs and sat down opposite him.

"You're on your way to London, Sadie tells me."

"Yeah."

"To work?"

"Yeah."

"Got a job lined up?"

"No."

He picked up one of Gerald's sport magazines and began to flip the pages over, all the while watching Kevin out of the corner of his eye. And Kevin was watching him and wondering. What did he want with Gerald? Gerald was settling in well enough at the farm, living a rather uneasy truce with Halliday and Maxton it was true, but at least they were avoiding outright trouble and after work he went off to the stables each day where he spent a couple of hours that he really enjoyed.

"Gerald not coming yet?" asked Doyle.

"He'll not be in for an hour or two."

"Don't mind if I hang on, do you?"

"What do you want with Gerald?" asked Kevin levelly.

Doyle shrugged. "Just passing. Your aunt gave me your address, thought I might as well look him up." He grinned. "Why, are you frightened I might kidnap him?"

Kevin did not bother to reply. He got up and went to the kitchen where Sadie was banging pots.

"Am I supposed to feed that character?"

"I'd never like to think I'd refuse hospitality to anyone," said Kevin.

"O.K."

She set the table and then called them to come and eat. Doyle came behind Kevin. He was hungry, ate everything put before him. He had probably no money, thought Sadie, eyeing him, and she hoped that Gerald would not be stupid enough to give him any. Gerald had managed to save a pound or two; it was for something special, he said, but would not tell them what. He came in when they were in the middle of their meal. He was quite taken aback by Jimmy Doyle's appearance and had obviously had no idea at all that he might turn up. He kept shaking his head and saying what a surprise it was.

After Gerald had eaten, the two boys went into the sitting room whilst Sadie and Kevin washed the dishes in the kitchen. A few minutes later Gerald looked in to say that he and Jimmy were going out for a bit. He hesitated.

"Could Jimmy stay the night, do you think? He'd sleep on the settee."

"I suppose so," said Kevin.

"Thanks," said Gerald. "Only for one night."

He and Doyle went off on the motor bike, Gerald without a crash hat, in spite of Kevin warning him that it was not only dangerous but against the law.

"The law!" said Doyle. "Sure we're not afraid of those gits. They'd never get the hold of us!"

"He's full of brave words that one," said Sadie, after they had gone.

"Things are coming back to me," said Kevin. "I'm sure he's been in Borstal."

"Don't tell me any more! You don't need to. It was a case of instant dislike."

They spent a restless evening. Sadie tried to knit but gave up; they watched television but started at every sound outside.

"Can you imagine what it'll be like when we're waiting for Brendan to come in?" said Sadie. "You know it mightn't be a bad thing if the police did stop them. Teach them a lesson."

But at eleven they heard the roar of the motor bike in the road. Gerald looked frozen; he had not been wearing heavy enough clothes. He hunched by the fire shivering. The breath of both boys was laden with beer. Kevin started to say something and then stopped. What was the point?

"Jimmy wants me to go to London with him," said Gerald, when Doyle had gone upstairs to the bathroom.

"London!" said Kevin.

"You'd be daft to go as far as the bend in the road with him," said Sadie. "Though you've been, so you are daft, aren't you?"

"Do you want to go, Gerald?" asked Kevin.

"I'm not sure. I'm not crazy about this place you know. Oh, it's all right in some ways but ould Halliday and Maxton get me down a bit at times. Neither of them like me, they're both waiting to get me. Now you can't deny that! They'd like fine to see me packing my bags."

"I wouldn't give them the satisfaction then," said Sadie.

"And London might be O.K.," said Gerald. "For a bit at any rate."

"With Doyle to keep you on the straight and narrow?" said Sadie. "You've got to be joking! He'd have you in Wormwood Scrubs before you could wink."

They heard the bathroom door open overhead.

"You'd be a fool to go anywhere with the likes of him, Gerald," said Kevin quietly. "But that's up to you."

Chapter Twelve

JIMMY DOYLE was up early. Sadie and Kevin heard him moving around downstairs when they wakened. They lay and listened.

"Sounds like he's in the kitchen," said Sadie.

"Probably making a cup of tea."

"Getting ready to leave maybe."

The bottom stair creaked. Doyle was coming up. He went into Gerald's room and closed the door. They heard voices, low and quiet at first, gradually becoming louder. Doyle's was raised above Gerald's.

Sadie slid out of bed and opened their door a crack.

"Sadie!"

"Sure we need to know what's going on." She put her ear to the opening.

"Ah for dear sake, you make me sick!" That was Doyle. "Are you intending to spend the rest of your life in this dump mucking out barns and doing what big brother tells you?"

"The cheek of him!" said Sadie, eyes flaring.

"I'm not intending to stay here for ever," said Gerald. "But it suits me well enough in the meantime. No, I'm going back to Ireland. One of these days."

Sadie closed the door. "Gerald's not going to London. He says he's going back to Ireland. One of these days."

Kevin sighed.

"You'd like to too, wouldn't you?" Sadie shivered. Her feet were perishing on the cold linoleum.

"I still feel we're exiles, Sadie."

"But how could we go back?" Sadie sat down on the edge of the bed. "With you Catholic and me Protestant and Brendan caught in the middle?"

"It's all right. There's no call for you to look so gloomy. I've no intention of going back at present. We might have to put up with being exiles all our lives. A lot of Irish do. Perhaps though we could go to Dublin sometime. They wouldn't bother there about you being Protestant."

"To live?"

"Why not?"

Sadie muttered something inaudible and began to dress. She would not fancy Dublin, not with all those priests running everywhere, and nearly everybody a Catholic. It was a Catholic country, whatever way she looked at it, and she could not stomach the idea of living in one.

There were footsteps on the stairs again, one pair. Doyle was going down. Sadie went to the window, pulled the curtain aside. The front door slammed, and she saw Doyle emerge on to the path below. He went round the side of the house for his bike. He rode off without a backward glance.

"Good riddance to bad rubbish!" said Sadie.

Kevin came up behind her, put his hands on her shoulders. "Don't worry now, Sadie love. I'll not be taking you anywhere you wouldn't want to go. Anyway, aren't we making a good life for ourselves here?"

Sadie nodded. "Yes, we are."

Gerald was quiet at breakfast. He said nothing about Doyle leaving, neither did they, though Sadie was dying to ask Gerald if he'd given Doyle any money. The postman brought Kevin a letter from his sister Brede to tell them that she had just had a baby girl. She had a boy one year old already. Everyone was fine, she said, though there had been a bomb explosion in the nearby village the week before and she worried when her husband Robert went to the pub for a drink. But it was not often he did go, and she herself and her mother seldom left the farm. She sent love to Sadie and Gerald and hoped all went well with them.

Kevin was quiet after he had folded the letter and put it away. What was he thinking of, Sadie wondered. Home?

But this was their home, she told herself after the brothers had gone to work and she was clearing up the dishes. She was going to do everything she could to make it a real one. She was going to grow vegetables in the garden once spring came and the ground was ready for a new planting. That way they would have all their own fresh vegetables and save money at the same time. And she would keep chickens and perhaps ducks. She had told Kevin so the night before. "Do you know anything about them?" he had asked. No, she knew nothing, but she could learn. She would learn. Mrs Maxton would teach her, tell her what to do, how to buy chickens. She might even be able to sell some eggs, make a little extra money. They could be doing with some; there were so many things they still needed in the house.

She was brisk and full of energy this morning. The sun had come out, dispersing the early morning mist, and when she had done her housework she was going to walk to the village. Brendan sat propped up in his pram watching her tidy the rooms. She dressed him warmly and set off.

The air was crisp and cold but invigorating, and the trees stood clearly out against the blue and white sky. They had had a lot of wet and misty weather since they had come so Sadie found it marvellous to see everything outlined so sharply. She had never known that bare trees could look so nice. She enjoyed the walk thoroughly. Brendan enjoyed it too, bouncing along in the pram, sometimes almost hitting the roof as they went over a pothole, gurgling when they did.

"You are going to be a country boy," Sadie told him. "Strong and healthy with rosy red cheeks. You'll run across the fields and climb trees. No dirty streets for you, my boyo!"

The old woman who lived in the first cottage in the village was cleaning her letter box.

"Good morning, Mrs Haughton," said Sadie. "Lovely day."

"Very nice." Mrs Haughton put down her Brasso tin and

duster on the step and had a look at Brendan. "My, he's growing!" They had a pleasant chat about babies—Mrs Haughton had ten grandchildren—and then Sadie moved on to the shop.

There was a girl serving today. Usually Mr Carter who owned it was behind the counter.

"Haven't seen you before," said Sadie.

"I live in the next village. I just started this morning." Her name was Pauline and she was the same age as Sadie. She had long brown hair down to her waist and big brown eyes. She laughed a lot. Brendan laughed, watching her. She and Sadie talked for nearly an hour until Brendan finally grew restless.

"Have you a boyfriend, Pauline?" asked Sadie. "Well, why don't you bring him along to our house one evening to meet my husband Kevin? We could have a bit of supper."

"That'd be lovely."

They fixed a day.

"See you," said Sadie.

It was nearing lunchtime. She had left the boys' meal in the oven and told them she might not be back. She opened a packet of rusks and put one into Brendan's hand. A coke and a sandwich was a fine idea for herself, even though she felt guilty spending money they could not afford. But she didn't spend much on herself, she reasoned, she bought few clothes and hardly any make-up.

She carried Brendan into the pub.

Mrs Hughes's face was flushed with excitement, "Sadie, come and see! Megan has had her pups." Megan was the Hughes's golden labrador.

The dog was in the kitchen with her pups. Sadie squatted beside the basket.

"They're gorgeous," she cried. "Absolutely gorgeous!" She had never seen such beautiful puppies. They looked like soft pieces of golden fluff as they lay curled round their mother. Megan raised proud eyes to Sadie, awaiting approval. "What a clever dog you are." Sadie stroked the dog's head gently. "Six of them! I could only produce one, Megan." Sadie had never seen puppies so young before. Hardly anyone in her street in Belfast had had a dog, except for the men who kept greyhounds and walked the thin whippets close beside them on a tight leash. She had always hated the sight of those greyhounds: their thinness bothered her.

"Aren't they lovely?" Mrs Hughes crouched down beside Sadie. "I should have no difficulty getting rid of those."

"What a pity you can't keep them!"

"But I breed them to sell, Sadie."

Sadie went into the lounge to drink her coke and eat her sandwich. As she chewed she thought of the puppies. She would love to have one, really love to. The desire burned a hole in her. It was a long time since she had wanted anything so much. Except for Kevin. She grinned at Brendan. And, oh yes, she had wanted Brendan too, though she hadn't known what he would be like. But now she had the image of those puppies in her mind and she wanted one badly. A soft golden ball of fluff.

Mrs Hughes was still in the kitchen. Sadie tapped on the door and went in.

"How much will you be selling the puppies for, Mrs Hughes?" she asked.

"Quite a lot, Sadie. You see, it costs a lot, the stud fee and feeding them."

"I know. But how much?"

"Too much for you, I'm afraid, dear, if that's what you're thinking of. Thirty pounds."

"Thirty pounds. Oh well!"

"I'm sorry, love. I'd have liked to have given you one, really I would."

"Oh I wouldn't expect that ..."

Thirty pounds. The sum was in Sadie's head all the way home. She no longer saw the trees, the sun gilding the branches, the holly berries, the robins chirping from their perches. Brendan slept. How could she get thirty pounds, thirty *extra* pounds, so that she would drain nothing from their budget?

When Kevin came in she told him immediately about the puppies. "They're so sweet, Kevin. You'd love them."

"We might get ourselves a dog one of these days. I quite fancy having one. Good for the wee fella too."

Her heart swooped with hope. "What about one of the Hughes's?"

"I mean a mongrel, Sadie. We can't afford a pure-bred like those."

"If we got one I could breed dogs like Mrs Hughes."

"You know nothing about it."

"I could learn. Please Kevin, please!"

"But we haven't the money, silly! How could I lay hands on thirty pounds?"

Sadie studied all the old newspapers, sitting hunched over them, frowning. What was she doing, Kevin wanted to know. Trying to find ways of making money, she told him; there must be some way she could raise the money. If you wanted anything badly enough you could usually get it.

"Is that right?" said Kevin. "It's news to me."

Sadie went the next day to the pub to see the puppies again. She hung over the basket for a long time stroking Megan's silky fur and watching the puppies who were gradually gaining strength and moving more and more all the time. She returned daily to see them. After three days Mrs Hughes let her pick up the pups in turn. They yowled when she took them from their mother's warmth. She held them only a little while, then returned them. There was one with a very sweet face. "Like a pansy," said Sadie. It was Mrs Hughes's favourite too.

"She's perfectly made," said Mrs Hughes. "She would be a good bitch to breed from."

"Don't promise her to anyone yet," begged Sadie. "Please! I'm trying to find the money."

"Oh all right." Mrs Hughes smiled but did not look very convinced by the prospect of Sadie being a buyer.

Sadie returned home, completely preoccupied by the puppy. There was a letter from Maria waiting. She ripped it open. Maria said she could come out the week-end after next. "Great," said Sadie aloud. She paced the floor.

But the puppy now ... Maybe she could borrow the money

from Mrs Hignett. But no, that wouldn't do. Mrs Hignett probably couldn't spare that kind of money. And besides, she, Sadie, had solemnly promised Kevin that she would never again borrow money, buy things on tick, or hire purchase, without discussing it with him first. When they had first been married she had kept buying things through clubs, paying them up weekly, and they had got into a terrible mess over money. She was still tempted at times for when she saw something nice she wanted it, and money had always burned a hole in her pocket, but she knew that Kevin would be so upset that the thought of it always stopped her.

She lamented the fact that she had no money to Pauline.

"Suppose it is tough," said Pauline. "Wouldn't fancy being that hard up myself." Pauline bought something new to wear nearly every week. She gave her mother a small amount and spent the rest of her wages, which were not large, on clothes. "Don't suppose you could take a job either. Not with Brendan."

"Not out here, in the middle of the wilderness! What could I do?"

"You might be able to get some work on the farm come summer."

"Summer!" said Sadie. "That's far too late."

Pauline came with her boyfriend to visit them. George was a motor mechanic and drove a souped-up Mini painted black and white. He took Kevin for a run in it and as soon as they came back they had the bonnet up with Kevin holding a torch over George's head.

"Kevin's mad about machines," said Sadie. "He's always taking the tractor engine to bits. Mr Maxton says he's very useful."

"That's good." Pauline yawned. She was not much interested in the farm and Sadie did not expect her to be. She liked best to talk about clothes.

"Pity we can't go out for a drink. Couldn't Gerald baby-sit for you?"

Gerald looked up from the magazine he was reading. "It's O.K. with me."

The girls put on their coats and went out to Kevin and George.

"We thought we'd go for a drink," said Pauline.

"Fine," said George.

Sadie thought Kevin did not look too pleased. When he went into the kitchen to wash the grease from his hands she followed him.

"What's the matter? Don't you like George and Pauline?"

"Sure. They're fine." He bent over the sink.

"What is it then?"

"I've no money, Sadie. Nothing. How can we buy drinks?"

"What kind of life is it if we can't even go out for a drink once in a blue moon?"

"I'm sorry." He sighed, lifted the towel from the rail and dried his hands slowly.

"Oh it's not your fault." Sadie raked in the drawer for her purse. She had one pound left for her housekeeping which had to last for the next two days. She gave it to him. "We have to go now we've said."

They spent the pound that evening. It was easy enough to do. Kevin had to take his turn of buying drinks.

"We must do this again," said Pauline.

"Yes," said Sadie.

When she went to the 'Ladies' she slipped into the kitchen to have another quick look at the puppies. She stroked her favourite's head.

"Money!" said Sadie to Megan, who looked unperturbed. "It's a pain in the neck."

Pauline and George came back with them for supper and stayed till midnight. Kevin was yawning behind his hand before they left. His day started so early that they usually went to bed early.

"Hope we haven't kept you up," said Pauline.

"No, no," Sadie assured her. "We like company, don't we, Kev?"

"Yes, sure. It was nice of you to come."

Kevin fell asleep as soon as his head met the pillow; Sadie lay awake for a long time. Her mind would not stop racing.

And then, when the alarm clock went off in the morning, she could hardly open her eyes. She reached out and shut it off, feeling that it must be the middle of the night and a big mistake. But as soon as Kevin left the bed and she began to cool, her mind came alive again. The first thing in it was thirty pounds.

After breakfast she went to see Mrs Maxton.

"Do you make much money with your hens?"

"Not a lot, Sadie. You need a lot of hens to make any at all."

Sadie sighed. "There must be something I could do. I want to earn money, Mrs Maxton."

"There's always the big house. Mrs Willis the housekeeper is often looking for domestic help."

Domestic help! How Mrs Jackson would have laughed if she could have seen Sadie trudging up the drive to offer her services! Sadie could hear her mother's voice ringing in her ear. "You're the stupidest thing in a house I ever did see!" But then she'd come a long way since those days. She was quite house-proud now. She shook her head. She never thought she'd have seen the day when she could say that of herself, but it was different when the house was your own.

She had left Brendan with Mrs Maxton. She rang the bell at the big house and after a moment the butler opened the door. She asked for Mrs Willis and was told to wait. She supposed she should have gone to the back door, she had a habit of thinking of things when it was too late.

The butler reappeared. "Would you come this way please?"

She followed him through a wide polished hall along a corridor into the kitchen. The butler went away, saying that Mrs Willis would be along shortly. Sadie looked round. It was a large bright room with an Aga cooker and a large electric one as well. All for two people!

The door opened, in came Mrs Willis, small and plump and smiling. Sadie knew at once that she would get on with her. She told her who she was and that she was looking for work. Mrs Willis said they were always needing help, it was difficult to get enough and it was a big house, and she herself was run off her feet. One woman had left just the week before. Yes, she could take Sadie on for mornings to help with general cleaning. One pound twenty a morning. Would that suit?

Six pounds a week! Sadie jumped at the offer.

"When can I start? Tomorrow?"

"You're keen." Mrs Willis laughed.

'There's just one thing, Mrs Willis. Could I bring my baby with me? He'd sit in his pram and be no trouble at all to anybody."

"Well I don't know now. I'm not supposed to, you see. Mrs Ellersley doesn't like women coming to work with children. We've had one or two and it's never worked out. There was one child who used to scream and run about and Mrs Ellersley got terrible headaches. She gets headaches easily. And she's not very fond of children." Mrs Willis was not smiling any more. "It's a pity. I think you'd have suited me fine."

"But Brendan can't run about, he's not old enough. And he never screams. Honest, there's hardly ever a cheep out of him. He's the quietest child you could ever imagine. And I'd leave him out in the garden in his pram where he'd be out of the way. Really, Mrs Willis, you'd have nothing to worry about."

Mrs Willis thought for a moment. "Very well, we'll give it a try. But if there's any trouble you understand I'd have to ask you to leave?" She smiled again. "You've got the gift of the blarney right enough. I think you could talk yourself into anything!"

Sadie collected Brendan and went straight to the pub.

"Keep my puppy," she told Mrs Hughes. "I'll have the money in five weeks."

would wear her knees to the bone.

"Did you say they'd no children?" said Sadie. "It seems an awful big place to keep on just for the two of them."

"They have a lot of visitors. There are some staying at the moment."

Sadie was to start first in the Ellersleys' bedroom. It was huge, for a bedroom, with windows on two sides looking out over the parkland.

"You could almost have a dance in here," said Sadie.

Mrs Willis smiled. "I'll leave you to it then, Sadie."

Sadie's feet sank into the fluffy white carpet. Such luxury to walk on! She would have liked to roll on it, was tempted for a moment, but thought better not, not on her first morning. She made the twin beds, smoothing down the satin top covers. She wouldn't have all this silk and satin herself, it wasn't in her line, but the materials were very fine and the colours attractive. The bedroom was mostly olive green and white, and there were daffodils on the window sill. She tidied the dressing table and dusted it. Mrs Ellersley had every kind of cream and lotion under the sun, treatment for wrinkles, dry skin, sallow neck, brown blotches, premature signs of ageing, clogged pores. Sadie shook her head. Mrs Ellersley must be a bonny looking sight if she needed all that lot! They were in expensive jars and some had their lids off, left lying just as they had been used, exposed to the air. Sadie sniffed each one, trying out the different smells. Avocado. What on earth was that? It was green. Funny colour to be putting on your face.

She jumped when the door opened. The woman who came in was tall and thin with dense black hair (dyed, thought Sadie), and she wore a knitted blue wool suit. Mrs Ellersley presumably. Sadie eyed her, not knowing whether to say hello or not.

"You the new maid?" said Mrs Ellersley.

"Yes," said Sadie, surreptitiously setting down the avocado cream.

Mrs Ellersley took a fur coat from the wardrobe and drifted out again.

It must be a great life, Sadie supposed, slipping into fur coats, gliding about the passages, going for a drive. Though it would have its drawbacks too no doubt. A bit boring. Mrs Ellersley had looked rather bored. Still, she, Sadie, could be doing with a bit of fur coat treatment herself, she'd be prepared to cope with the boredom. There was a white fur cape lying on the back of a chair. She picked it up and slung it around her shoulders. She stood in front of a long mirror, hand on hip. "How do you do, Mrs McCoy?" She held out her hand languidly to an imaginary inquirer, palm downwards. A footstep in the corridor made her pull off the cape and return it quickly to the chair. The footsteps passed by; Sadie went back to her work.

She was vacuuming the carpet the next time the door opened.

"I'm afraid your baby's crying his eyes out," said Mrs Willis. "He's in a terrible state, poor wee lad."

It took Sadie ten minutes to pacify him. He cried so sorely that any passer-by would have thought he was being battered. Mrs Willis told Sadie to bring him in by the kitchen fire. This he seemed to prefer, and when he had quietened he looked about with interest.

"You'd better keep him inside with you this morning," said Mrs Willis. "He's obviously feeling strange. Mrs Ellersley's gone out. But you can't have him in every day, you know."

"No, no, I wouldn't expect to," said Sadie. "Thank you very much, Mrs Willis."

She carried Brendan from room to room with her, laying him on the bed or floor whilst she worked. He was good now, made no fuss.

"You little devil!" she said to him shaking her fist, and he laughed. "Oh aye, go on, laugh!"

She worked an extra half hour to make up for the time she had lost over Brendan.

"You seem to be a good worker, Sadie." Mrs Willis nodded her head with approval.

The next morning Sadie woke Brendan early, propped him

up in his pram and gave him toys to play with. "I'm trying to exhaust him," she told Kevin, "so that he'll be tired by nine and spend the morning sleeping."

"You hope! I'm not a bit keen on you doing this, you know, Sadie."

"Well, I'm going to do it. It's not just for the puppy. After I've paid for her I'll be able to buy us all sorts of other things too."

Brendan's head was drooping as she pushed him up the drive to the big house. He yawned. "Good boy, Brendan," she said. She parked the pram, laid him down. It was his signal to come back to life again. He was crying lustily before she got her coat off. She decided she would leave him, hoping that he might tire if he saw no good would come of it. Neither Mrs Jones nor Mrs Willis was in the kitchen to comment so she went quickly upstairs and began work. She had only made the first bed when Mrs Willis came looking for her.

"Your baby's crying."

Sadie brought him into the kitchen again. Mrs Willis was looking troubled.

"I wouldn't mind if you had him in, Sadie. But Mrs Ellersley—" She broke off as the door opened and Mrs Ellersley herself came in.

"Oh Mrs Willis, I'd like a word with you please." Her eyes flickered over the baby in Sadie's arms.

Mrs Willis followed her out into the hall.

"I think she's horrible," said Sadie.

"Oh she's all right," said Mrs Jones. "In her own way. Not very friendly, but she doesn't bother us much. And you can't blame her if she doesn't want kids making a noise in the house. It's her house after all."

"I suppose not." Sadie sighed, blaming her nevertheless, thinking of the little golden puppy.

"Kids get on her nerves. You see, she couldn't have any herself. Least, that's what I heard."

Mrs Willis came back. "Mrs Ellersley has been complaining about the baby crying. I'm afraid, Sadie—"

"I'll have to see if I can make other arrangements," said

Sadie miserably. "I'll try to get someone to look after Brendan." But who? She couldn't ask Mrs Maxton or Mrs Hughes, and she didn't know anyone else well enough.

She pushed the pram to the village and told Pauline her tale of woe.

"Leave him with me," said Pauline.

"In the shop?"

"Why not? He can sit in his pram and watch the people coming in and out. He'd like that."

Yes, he would, better than sitting outside the back door of the Ellersleys' house staring at the wall. Mr Carter the shopkeeper did not mind. It was no skin off his nose, he said. He was taking life easy, on doctor's orders, so he only came in to the shop for an hour or two each day, just to see that everything was all right.

Sadie arranged with Mrs Willis to begin work half an hour later as Pauline did not arrive in the village till nine.

"You see, there's always a way," said Sadie to Kevin over breakfast the following day.

"You'll kill yourself. You've got to push the pram to the village, go back to the house, work three hours and then walk to the village again to fetch him. And how are Gerald and I going to get our lunch?"

"I'll have to leave it for you to heat up," said Sadie sharply, defying him to object to that.

He shrugged, got up and fetched his jacket. "I know there's no stopping you, Sadie, not once you're bent on something!"

She managed everything perfectly, she told him in the evening, it had been no trouble at all. Brendan had behaved with Pauline and charmed all the customers and Mr Carter had said that Brendan was a grand wee chap.

"Mr Carter knows what it's like trying to manage," said Sadie. "But that Mrs Ellersley hasn't a clue. She's had a cook and a housekeeper and somebody making her bed all her life. She doesn't know anything about it."

"She might know a thing or two," said Kevin. "Different things. Oh, I don't know. I don't much care." He was taking a radio to bits and was more interested in that than Mrs

130

Ellersley. Women were never done talking about people, and it bored him. Gerald was out. He was seldom in at all these days; he spent his free hours in the stables, came home smelling of horses, his clothes covered in hairs, which made Sadie cluck. Why didn't he sleep there? she asked him.

On Friday Sadie was paid for the three mornings she had worked. The money meant more to her than any she had ever earned before. She walked to the village with it clutched in her hand.

"Look, Pauline!" cried Sadie. And Maria was coming for the week-end. Sadie went home singing.

When they met Maria off the bus she greeted them shyly, holding back a little, but once she had been in the house for half an hour everything was as it had been before. Brendan seemed to remember her too and sat on her knee trying to reach her curly hair with his restless fingers.

"He's terrible just now," said Sadie. "He won't stay still for a minute. He drives me up the wall!"

Maria laughed: "You'll have less and less peace now, Sadie."

Sadie groaned. "I'm beginning to see why my mother was never done moaning."

Gerald did not go to the stables at all over the week-end except when he took Maria to see the horses. He showed her round the farm on Saturday. Sadie lent her a pair of Wellingtons two sizes too large and a duffle coat. Maria looked like a little girl lost in the outfit.

"You can't go round in thin town stuff here, you know," said Sadie.

She watched Maria and Gerald go off.

"You sound like an old country hand these days," said Kevin.

"I'm beginning to feel like one too. You'll soon be able to pick the straw out of my ears."

She still missed the town, at least when she had time to think about it, and listening to Maria talk about the neighbours made her feel homesick. She longed for the sight of a city street with all its hustle and bustle and the feel of things happening.

"Things happen here too," said Kevin. "Cows'll be calfing next month."

"Cows!" said Sadie.

They would go up to Liverpool for a day as soon as they could afford it, Kevin promised, but the fares cost quite a lot and they would need money to spend too.

Sadie had a letter from Kitty that morning. She and Bill were busy on their house: they were painting the bathroom a delicate shade of shell pink and had bought deeper pink and black linoleum tiles for the floor. There followed a bit about the difficulties of laying lino tiles which Sadie skipped through hastily. She felt slightly depressed when she had finished reading the letter. Kitty seemed to be interested in nothing but her house these days.

Sadie sighed.

"What's up?" asked Kevin.

"People seem to come and go so easily. Well, there was Kitty—"

"You'll see her again."

"And Lara. Do you remember Lara?" Lara had been an Indian friend in London. "I wonder what's happened to her? I always seem to lose touch with people." With this mood upon her, she sat down and wrote to her brother Tommy who had gone to Australia. 'Please write soon and tell me all about yourself', she finished up.

They had a good week-end with Maria, and Sadie spent the extra three pounds and sixty pence. She could not resist a lovely big joint of beef when the butcher called in his van and the baker had a sumptuous chocolate cake and then there was fresh cream for the apple pie ... Oh well, it wasn't very often that they could afford such a spread. And it wasn't often they had a visitor.

Next week she would definitely put away every penny she earned for the pup.

Chapter Fourteen

NEXT WEEK it snowed. Sadie stood by the window cursing the drifting white flakes. They were fat and solid and determined to lie. Already the ground was covered, for it had begun to snow when they were going to bed the night before. The trees, shrouded in feathery white, looked beautiful. But Sadie was in no mood for beauty. She wanted to go to work.

When Kevin and Gerald came in for breakfast they said the road was almost impassable to the village; only vehicles with heavy tyres could make it, and she would certainly never get through with the pram. She did not argue, knowing that they were right. She had already gone a few yards along the road to test the depth of the snow.

"Will I stop by at the house and tell Mrs Willis?" asked Kevin.

"No, no," said Sadie. "I'm going to take Brendan in his carrycot. Will you help me carry him, Kev?"

Protesting, Kevin took the other side of the cot. She wasn't supposed to take Brendan at all, was she? But this was an emergency, claimed Sadie, due to severe weather conditions.

"Isn't that what you'd call it?" she said, grinning, as they set off floundering through the snow, slipping and sliding with the effort of carrying the cot between them. Snow blew against Brendan's face delighting him. He tried to catch the flakes on his blue woollen mitts.

"Mercy!" exclaimed Mrs Willis when she opened the back door and saw them standing there like ghosts. Kevin disappeared quickly saying he would come back for Sadie at twelve.

"I didn't want to let you down, Mrs Willis," said Sadie.

"All right, you can leave him in the kitchen!"

Brendan did not cry at all that morning. He lay in his carry-cot watching Mrs Jones peel vegetables and bake. She talked to him from time to time and eventually, with the heat of the fire, he dropped off to sleep.

"He's no trouble at all," said Mrs Jones to Mrs Willis. "Nice little chap. Bit of company for me too."

Sadie sang as she worked. Mrs Ellersley passed her in the corridor without a word. She looked as if she might not care for singing either. Sadie shrugged, switched on the vacuum and broke into song again. As she went from room to room she planned how she would arrange the house if it was hers and Kevin's. A nursery for Brendan, workshop for Kevin, general messing-around room for herself, and the room next to the kitchen would do nicely for the dogs.

She sailed into the library without realising that Mr Ellersley stood by the shelves with a book in his hand.

"Hello."

"Sorry." She backed out.

"It's all right. You won't disturb me. I'm just looking something up."

She began to dust the shelves.

"Lots of books to dust, I'm afraid," he said.

"Have you read them all?"

"Most of them." He replaced the book, turned to go. "I didn't know you were working in the house. What's your name again?"

"Sadie. Sadie McCoy."

"Ah yes. Your husband's doing well, I hear. And your brother-in-law is never out of the stables."

"I hope he's not making a nuisance of himself?"

"Not at all. He's got a good eye for a horse, handles them well too. Well, must go, I've got business in Chester. Goodbye Sadie."

"Goodbye," she said.

There were several pictures of horses in the library, elegant stream-lined racehorses, some with jockeys on their backs, some standing alone. There were paintings and photographs of horses all over the house. Sadie liked the look of horses herself but she liked them best in the fields when they were cropping grass or galloping, riderless, their manes and tails streaming in the wind.

The snowy spell lasted all week. Each morning Kevin helped Sadie to carry Brendan to the house and collected them again at lunch-time. Sadie said it was working out fine: Mrs Willis and Mrs Jones were happy, Brendan was happy, and Mrs Ellersley did not know.

Mr Halliday's back was troubling him even more in this weather and his temper, never of the easiest, was frayed to the edges. He tolerated Kevin now, seldom called him to task for indeed there was little fault that he could find with his work, but he watched every move that Gerald made, pouncing on his slightest mistake. Often Gerald gave him cause to complain, coming late for milking, idling around. He spent too much time at the stables, Kevin told him; he should not go there in working hours.

"But it's only the horses that keep me going," said Gerald.

The rows between him and Halliday continued to build up. They were often small and niggling, usually starting over a petty offence, but it was obvious to Kevin that eventually there must be a real blow up. And there was.

Gerald did not arrive at all one afternoon for the second milking. Kevin carried on, annoyed with Gerald who always pushed things too far in the end and tried people's patience beyond the point where they had any left. Halliday certainly had none now. He gave Kevin a hand, puffing and complaining about his back, even though Kevin had said he could manage alone. But Mr Halliday enjoyed being a martyr and Kevin was not going to deprive him of his pleasure.

"He can't go on like this. It's no way to keep down a job."

"He's still young, Mr Halliday. He'll steady up yet."

"Seventeen! I started at fourteen years of age, up every morning at four...."

Kevin had heard before the story of Mr Halliday's youth. A lot of people's youth was hard, even now, Kevin wanted to tell him, but there was no point in wasting breath. Mr Halliday would not listen.

They closed the cans, stacked them on the truck. Mr Halliday groaned from the pain in his back, putting his hand to it.

"Here he comes, the brave lad! Look at him, taking his time as if he was lord of the manor!"

Gerald deliberately slackened speed as soon as he saw that he was observed. He slouched into the barn, hands in pockets. Mr Halliday embarked on his tirade. When he paused, Gerald said, "I was helping out at the stables. One of the horses was foaling and Mr Wright was away. Bobby was on his own."

"I don't give a damn about the horses. It's the cows I'm bothered about."

"But the vet hadn't come and the horse was having trouble—"

"We were having trouble." Mr Halliday spat on the ground. He called Gerald a few names and told him he wasn't worth his wage. "You're nothing but a useless layabout."

"And you're nothing but a stupid ould git," said Gerald. "I wouldn't work for you if I was starving." He turned and walked off.

"You needn't think you'll have a chance to work for me again," Mr Halliday called after him. "Oh, not that I imagine you'll starve. You'll live off your brother!"

So Gerald got his books. As Mr Maxton said to Kevin, he had no alternative but to sack Gerald after the way he had carried on and insulted Mr Halliday. "You must admit he's not killed himself working either has he, Kevin?"

Kevin could not say otherwise. He went home to tell Sadie.

"So what do we do now?" she demanded. "Keep him? As if he was a baby like Brendan. And here am I working my guts out to make a bit of extra money and now we'll need it just to live."

"I don't know what to do," said Kevin. "If I put him out he might go after Doyle."

"I'm sick of being nursemaid to your brother." Sadie flounced up the stairs to the bedroom. To think that she might not get her puppy now and it would be Gerald's fault! She came back downstairs and said, "There's some people you can't help. It's like knocking your head against a brick wall."

"If you want, Sadie, I'll tell him to go."

"Great! And then it'd be on my head."

Gerald came in late. He'd get another job, he said, he didn't intend to sponge off them.

"Doing what?" asked Sadie.

Sadie was dusting the staircase and keeping an eye on the library which was directly in her line of vision below. Mr Ellersley had not left the dining room yet; she had seen him, when she passed the half-open door, sitting at the table, his chair pushed back from it a bit to allow him to cross his legs, reading the newspaper. He nearly always went to the library after breakfast to deal with his correspondence.

Mrs Willis came along the top landing with her firm, measured tread, carrying a pile of newly laundered sheets. "No need to do that today, Sadie," she said.

"It's needing a clean, Mrs Willis." Sadie ran a finger along the top of a heavy gilt-framed picture, then held it up to show the grime. "See!"

"All right, but don't take long. I want you to give the drawing room a good turn out today."

Sadie studied the picture in the frame. It was a dark painting, heavy with thick browns and greens, so that, close-up, she could make out little of what it was about. Standing back, she saw that it was a country scene, with two trees hanging over a brook, and from the colours, she decided it must be November.

"Do you like it?" said a voice below. It was Mr Ellersley's.

She almost fell backwards down the stairs. She recovered balance and leaning against the balustrade, looked down at him.

"Not much, to be honest. It doesn't do anything for me.

Do you like it?"

"Yes, I do." He smiled. He went into the library, closing the door behind him.

She turned and had another look at the picture. This time she made out a little more, saw other colours reflected in the water. She supposed it wasn't bad. Swiftly but carefully she dusted round it, then skimmed her duster down the banister to the bottom.

She opened the library door and went in. "Am I disturbing you?" she asked meekly.

"No. Just carry on, Sadie."

She dusted one shelf of thick leather spines with the titles written in gold script. Charles Dickens. She had read one or two of them at school and found them heavy going. Mr Ellersley was sitting at his desk writing. She moved nearer, and when he glanced up, she spoke.

"Mr Ellersley—"

"Yes?"

"I don't suppose you need another hand in the stables?" she blurted out quickly. She had rehearsed what she would say whilst she was making the beds and fiddling around on the stairs; now, in the heat of the moment, it had gone from her. She had meant to be more subtle, lead up to it, mention it casually, as it were.

"Why?" He was amused. "Are you looking for a job?"

"Oh not for me. It's Gerald. You see, he got his books from Mr Maxton for calling Mr Halliday a stupid ould git. But, honestly, Mr Halliday is—" She stopped.

"If you could just slow down, Sadie, and tell me what happened."

She put down her duster and he invited her to take a chair. She pulled up a green leather armchair on the other side of the desk. She told him all about Gerald, the trial he had been to his family, and to her and Kevin, and how he had grown up amidst the violence of Belfast.

"You see, Mr Ellersley, he's never had much of a chance. He wouldn't have had any at all if Kevin hadn't taken him in."

"He's a good man, that one of yours."

"Yes, I know that full well."

Mr Ellersley fiddled with his pen, turning it between his fingers. "I'll need to think about it, Sadie. You see, Mr Maxton and Mr Halliday wouldn't be pleased, and I have to consider them."

"But the stables have nothing to do with them."

"Yes, but even so.... And there's another thing, can I be sure that Gerald will do his job properly there when he didn't on the farm?"

"But he's mad on horses. And good with them. You've said so yourself. That would make all the difference."

"Yes, you're probably right about that. But there's still Mr Maxton." Mr Ellersley pursed his lips. "I'll think about it, Sadie, I promise."

She stood up. "All right, thanks, Mr Ellersley. And I'd be grateful if you wouldn't mention to Gerald or Kevin that I spoke to you about it. Kevin would be right mad at me. He doesn't like asking for things but sometimes I think you've got to."

"I think you're right, Sadie. When it's important. And this is."

Sadie met Mrs Willis as she was leaving the library.

"Where have you been, girl? You'll never get that drawing room done today. It takes ages dusting all those little china figures of Mrs Ellersley's."

"I'll do extra time, Mrs Willis."

"Yes, I know you will. You're good that way. I've no complaints about your work. Come and get your coffee before you start."

Brendan was sitting up eating a biscuit, or rather, sucking it, for he had no teeth as yet.

"My toothless wonder!" Sadie bent down to kiss the top of his head. "Have you been a good boy then?"

"Very good," said Mrs Jones. "Not a cheep out of him."

Sadie drank a cup of coffee with Mrs Jones and Mrs Willis by the fire.

"What a nice man Mr Ellersley is!" said Sadie.

"You were in there talking to him, weren't you?" said Mrs Willis. "I thought I heard your voice. What a girl!"

The door opened. They looked round.

"Ah, Mrs Willis!" said Mrs Ellersley. Her eyes moved from the group at the fire to where Brendan sat in his carrycot on the floor. He waved his biscuit in the air and gurgled. "I wanted to see you about the guest rooms, Mrs Willis."

Mrs Willis put down her cup, followed Mrs Ellersley out.

"What a bit of luck!" groaned Sadie.

"She was bound to find out sooner or later," said Mrs Jones complacently. "But I wouldn't worry. Mrs Willis'll speak up for you."

Chapter Fifteen

"MRS ELLERSLEY's agreed to let me have Brendan in the kitchen while I'm working," said Sadie.

"That's a queer turnabout, isn't it?" said Kevin. "What came over her?"

"Mrs Willis," Sadie giggled. "She threatened to go on strike if she didn't let me. Mrs Ellersley wanted to give me the sack but Mrs Willis put her foot down. She told her a thing or two, so she said. And Mrs Jones is quite happy to keep an eye on Brendan. She's very fond of him. He's a real charmer."

"Or you are!"

Sadie grinned. "More soup?"

"Wouldn't mind."

Sadie put another ladleful of thick broth on to his plate. Gerald had not come in for lunch and Kevin did not know where he was.

"Snow's melting," said Kevin. "If only Gerald could get settled! He's a real worry to me."

"Maybe something'll turn up."

"What?" asked Kevin gloomily.

Sadie closed her mouth up tight. It was all that she could do to stop herself from telling him about her talk with Mr Ellersley. When Kevin had gone back to work she told Brendan who was chewing the ear of a fluffy blue rabbit.

"You're useful for telling things to aren't you?" Brendan gurgled approval. "Yes, you are, you're good at keeping a secret. But that won't last for long I suppose."

On Friday she took her wages straight to the village. She laid five pounds in a row on Mrs Hughes' kitchen table. She was keeping one to buy a piece of meat for their Sunday dinner.

"That's the first instalment on the pup," she said.

Mrs Hughes gathered up the money and put it in a tin on the mantlepiece. "You seem to be determined, Sadie."

"Oh I am!" Sadie lifted the puppy from the basket and cuddled it against her. "She knows she's mine. Look how sweet she is! She'll be a great playmate for Brendan."

By Monday the snow had gone and she was able to push Brendan up to the house in his pram again. She saw a flash of white on the grass beside the drive and stopped. A snowdrop. She picked it. "Look, Brendan, a flower." He held out his hand for it but she did not give it to him for he would have mangled it. It would die quickly enough anyway. "I shouldn't have picked it, Brendan, but I couldn't resist it. The first spring flower. And soon there'll be crocuses. Yellow and purple. Won't that be lovely?"

She was on tenterhooks as soon as she entered the house. She threw her coat on a chair and sped along the corridor. The dining room door was open, the remains of breakfast lay on the table, but no one was there. She cleared the table and carried the dirty dishes to the kitchen.

"They're finished early this morning," she said to Mrs Jones. "Usually Mr Ellersley likes to sit a bit over his break-fast."

"He had to go to Chester this morning."

She kept an eye on the drive every time she went into a room at the front of the house but there was no sign of his car before she had finished. She hovered about in the kitchen afterwards until Mrs Willis told her she'd better get a move on or Brendan would be starving. He was gnawing hungrily at his rabbit's ear.

As Sadie reached the bottom of the drive Mr Ellersley's car

turned into it. A smile lit up her face. She felt he must be going to say yes. It was too good a day for anything bad to happen.

He stopped the car, wound down the window. "Lovely day, Sadie."

"Gorgeous."

The sun was shining brilliantly and somewhere nearby a bird was chirping. Sadie waited, her hands clenched tightly round the handle of the pram.

"I've thought about Gerald," said Mr Ellersley. "And I've spoken to Mr Maxton."

"Yes?"

"He says he doesn't mind one way or the other. As long as he doesn't have Gerald back working for him." Mr Ellersley grinned briefly. "So I've decided to give Gerald a chance to see how he can make out in the stables."

Sadie whooped with delight. Mr Ellersley drove off up to the house.

Gerald came home for tea smiling.

"I've been offered a job in the stables," he said.

"Have you?" Kevin was astonished.

"Are you taking it?" jumped in Sadie.

" 'Deed I am. I start tomorrow." Gerald could not stop grinning. "I can't get over it."

"Well isn't that great?" said Kevin.

"Marvellous," said Sadie. She turned to Brendan and winked. "I suppose then, Gerald, I'll have you coming home smelling of horses all the time?"

"Seems you will."

Gerald was off at dawn in the morning and every other morning. He came home only to eat.

More snowdrops flowered, and then the crocuses thrust their spikes up through the dark earth. Sadie watched over them carefully, discovering new ones each day. Each one seemed like a miracle. She had never watched a spring come like this before for she had always lived in cities. Belfast, London, Liverpool. And now here she was in the middle of the country where things were moving, growing, changing daily. She had not imagined so much going on. The branches of the trees were becoming flecked with buds of the lightest green. She saw hares scampering madly in the field behind their house. And the birds were returning, filling the air with their song, pleasing Brendan when he sat out in his pram in the garden.

It was a busy time for Kevin for the cows were calving, and right in the middle of it Mr Halliday had to go off to hospital to have an operation on his back. Fortunately, they had just taken on another boy. So Kevin came home late and Sadie was often on her own again. The lengthening evenings made her feel restless: it seemed a time to be out and not in the house. But she could not leave Brendan. She wanted too to have the day in Liverpool that they had promised themselves but now Kevin could not take the time off. He would, he said, as soon as things eased. Maria wrote a long letter full of news, sending greetings from her mother, Mrs Hignett, the Fiskes and everyone else they had known. But Maria could not come for another visit at the moment. She would though, as soon as she could. She sent her regards to Gerald.

"Brendan," said Sadie, "I never seem to have everything I want at the one time."

Brendan did: he was content.

The days, and weeks, passed quickly. Each Friday Sadie went to the village and gave Mrs Hughes another instalment, usually five pounds, never less than four.

"I've only two pounds to go," she told Kevin and Gerald one Friday lunchtime as she served their meal. "So this time next week we'll have a dog in the family."

Gerald got up and went upstairs. He returned after a minute and laid two pounds on the table.

"What's that for?" asked Sadie.

"The pup."

"Gerald!" Sadie flung her arms round his neck. Gerald went red in the face and Kevin laughed.

Sadie put on her coat at once. She could not wait to eat now. Food at a time like this!

"See you later!" she called, and was out with the pram, running almost, along the road to the village. She was breathless when she reached the pub.

"Mrs Hughes, I've got it," she gasped. "The money!"

"Well, well!" Mrs Hughes, who had been having her lunch, got up from the table smiling. "I'm really pleased for you, dear." She knelt down, lifted the puppy from the basket and put it into Sadie's arms.

The puppy licked Sadie's face all over, wagging its tail frantically.

"You'd think she knew," laughed Sadie.

"Oh I think she must have a good idea," said Mrs Hughes. "What are you going to call her?"

"Tamsin."

Sadie carried Tamsin all the way home in her arms. She was afraid to put her on the pram in case she would try to jump down and she did not want to let her walk in case it would tire her.

"Now you mustn't be soft with her," said Kevin. "That wouldn't be being kind to the beast. You have to train her properly from the start."

"But she's only little." Sadie stroked the silky ears.

Brendan, who had been watching closely, suddenly crumpled up his face and started to cry.

" 'Deed I believe he's jealous," cried Kevin, lifting him up. Brendan looked over his father's shoulder at Sadie and his lip trembled.

Sadie laughed, put down the dog and held her arms out for Brendan. His face cleared at once. "Petted lump!" she said. "But you'll have to get used to the competition."

After a few days Brendan adored Tamsin and could not have too much of her. They rolled about on the floor together. Everywhere that Sadie and Brendan went Tamsin went with them. Except to work. Mrs Willis was adamant about that. "You can't bring a dog with you, Sadie. I have to draw the line at that. I don't care how sweet it is or how good." So Sadie left Tamsin in the kitchen with food and water whilst they were gone. The dog was heart-broken whenever they shut the door on her. Sadie had to walk away quickly. "She'll be all right in a minute, Brendan." Tamsin usually chewed everything she could reach before they came back so they had to leave her a supply of old boots and shoes.

Sadie took Brendan to see the calves. They were beautiful, barely able to stand, with soft eyes. Kevin let Brendan stroke one although Brendan would have preferred to do something livelier like grasp its ear. Kevin looked very much at home in the barn moving amongst the cows. He was also at home with the farm machinery and he spent a part of each day working on it.

"Cowman and mechanic!" he said. "That's me. I like the two things. They're a change from one another."

Sadie took Brendan to see the horses and their foals too. Gerald held the horses' heads to let Brendan have a better look but these were beasts he could not touch. They were highly strung, nervous animals, stepping high and daintily in their stable. Sadie admired the foals and the calves, was enchanted by them, but there was nothing to beat her boisterous, loving puppy.

"You were worth the thirty pounds, Tamsin, every bit of it. And when you are full grown I'm going to let you have pups and I'll sell them and make money."

Sadie spent her next week's wages on a second-hand settee. She saw it advertised in *The Chester Chronicle* and Kevin fetched it on one of the farm Land Rovers. They took the old one out to the back garden and burnt it.

"Can't say I'm sorry to see the last of that," said Kevin, as they stood enjoying the glow of the bonfire.

"Smell the last of it, you mean," said Sadie. "Now that it's gone I'm prepared to admit it did pong a little."

She was saving now for a car. "Just a little one," she said. "Second-hand of course."

"It'll need to be very little and ancient," said Kevin "or we'll be waiting till Domesday. There's the tax and insurance too, you know." But he was in favour of saving for a car for then they could go out in the summer time, the three of them, or four, if Gerald wanted to join them. "Five," Sadie corrected him. They could go exploring in Wales. They had heard that North Wales was beautiful. They were only a few miles from the border but without their own transport it was difficult to go very far. Sadie borrowed a map from Mr Ellersley so that they could see where they might go.

"Fancy borrowing a map from him!" Kevin shook his head.

"But he and I are friends. He was only too pleased to lend it to me."

Mr Ellersley would not take it back when she offered it. "No, no, Sadie, I've got plenty of maps. In fact, I've looked out a few more of Cheshire, Derbyshire—the Peak district is beautiful too—and the Yorkshire moors. There are no lack of places to go from here."

"There's only a lack of money," said Sadie to Kevin.

Mr Halliday was discharged from hospital and told he must retire. His back would stand no more hard work. So Kevin was promoted to head cowman, and his wage increased.

"This calls for a celebration," said Sadie. "Where are you taking me?"

He took her to Chester for a meal and to the cinema afterwards. Gerald looked after Brendan.

"Sure Gerald has his uses," said Sadie, as they were coming home on the bus. "And now I'm used to him around the house I don't mind him a bit."

"Good." Kevin held Sadie's hand in his. He looked out at the dark night beyond the bus windows and smiled.

And then Kitty and Bill made their long-awaited visit. The garden was full of tulips, hyacinths and primulas. Sadie took Kitty on a conducted tour round the paths.

"Very nice," said Kitty.

"I'll give you a bunch of flowers to take home. And come and see where I've planted my potatoes." Sadie led the way round the back.

"My goodness, Sadie, you're turning into a right country bumpkin!"

"I like growing things. It's great seeing them come up."

"I suppose it is," said Kitty dubiously.

Sadie laughed. "It's a marvellous life."

"But don't you miss people?" Kitty gazed at the fields stretching away behind the cottage, with not another human being but themselves in sight.

"I've got Brendan and Tamsin."

"A baby and a dog. They're not people, I mean, to talk to."

"I talk to them all the time."

Kitty looked at Sadie as if she had gone a bit soft in the head.

"And I've got Mrs Willis and Mrs Jones at the big house where I work. I talk to them. And the girl in the shop."

"But that's a couple of miles away isn't it?" Kitty shivered. The sun was shining but the wind was sharp.

Sadie extolled the virtues and benefits of country life, refusing to admit to Kitty that she did indeed miss people at times and there were moments when she was alone with Brendan and it was dark or raining when she longed to be able to run along the street to Mrs Hignett's shop. It came over her in waves; sometimes it bothered her, sometimes it did not.

"Could we go inside?" said Kitty. "It's a bit chilly out here."

"Yes, come on in. I've a lovely log fire going for you. We get all the logs free. D'you know, Kitty, I wouldn't go back to the town if you paid me?"

What a lot of lies she told at times, thought Sadie; or at least, she often said things that she was not really sure of, certainly not as sure as she sounded. She might well be prepared to go back to the city if circumstances were right, she didn't feel that strongly against it, but Kitty looked so disapproving that it made Sadie desperate to have her admire their cottage and garden, to say something that might suggest she was even slightly envious. Just a little bit. But of course how could Kitty be envious when she had such a desirable three-bedroomed semi and ever such nice neighbours?

"You must miss having neighbours," said Kitty.

"Not really," said Sadie, trying to sound as if things like that were beneath her.

"Anyway, it's super to see you again, Sadie, it really is. I've missed you a heck of a lot. We'd have come ages ago if we hadn't been so busy with the house."

"It's super to see you too, Kitty."

And it was, and they had a good day, the four of them together again. This was what Sadie missed most: being with another couple of their own age, talking and laughing, eating and drinking. It made her feel warm and gay. Pauline and George came in occasionally but they liked to be out and about and after they'd sat down for an hour they wanted to be off again. They liked to spend money too, which Kevin and Sadie could not afford to do.

"Come and see us when you get your car," said Kitty and Bill before they left.

"When," said Sadie, after they had driven away. The house seemed quiet and empty now.

"What's up with you?" asked Kevin.

"Nothing." She went to the kitchen and began to wash the dishes. He followed her.

"What is it?"

"Oh it's just that we never seem to be able to get away from this place. I like it but there are times—" She sighed. "There are times when I wish we were back in Liverpool, slums and all."

Kevin was quiet, then he said, "Let's go up to Liverpool next Saturday."

Chapter Sixteen

"WELL, FOR goodness sake!" exclaimed Mrs Hignett. "Sadie and Kevin! I'd given up hope of ever laying eyes on the two of you again."

"We were hoping to see you at our place, Mrs Hignett."

"Oh I meant to come, love. But you know what it's like." Mrs Hignett turned her eyes on Brendan whom Kevin carried on his arm. "And is that the boy? What a size he is! Come and see your auntie then!" She held out her arms. Brendan looked at her for a moment unblinkingly, then decided he wanted nothing to do with being passed like a parcel to a stranger. He buried his face against Kevin's chest. Liverpool and its people had no place in his memory. "Ah well never mind, maybe later," said Mrs Hignett. She suddenly realised that Sadie was carrying something in her arms too. "Is that a dog you have there, Sadie?"

"Tamsin." Sadie held her up and Tamsin, hearing her name, barked appreciatively and wriggled to be released. Sadie set her down on the floor and she scurried round the back of the counter to investigate, trailing her leash behind her.

"For dear sake!" Mrs Hignett jumped as the dog rushed between her feet snuffling at her ankles. She was unused to animals, and unsure of them. She eyed Tamsin with apprehension. "It's got plenty of energy for the size of it."

"She's absolutely brilliant," said Sadie. "Pure-bred too. You should see her pedigree! I'm going to breed from her."

Mrs Hignett was astonished by the very idea. Sadie launched forth enthusiastically on the breeding of dogs. She and Mrs Hughes never talked about anything else now and Sadie had got several books out of the library.

"She's full of big ideas, Mrs Hignett," said Kevin.

"Better that than little ones," said Sadie, going round the back of the counter to catch Tamsin who had scented a few appetising things.

"You're right there, love," said Mrs Hignett. "Think big!"

She took them through to the back for a cup of tea and called in Mrs Fiske to come and have a look at Brendan. The women started to gossip, about this one who had married, that one who had had a baby, what Mrs So-and-So had said ... Kevin said he thought he'd go for a walk.

He wondered where Gerald had gone. He had come with them from the farm but had left them at the station saying he had shopping to do.

Kevin turned into their old street and walked as far as their house. The windows of their flat were boarded over. So no one had followed them. He was glad, for the place had not been fit for human beings. Mrs Francie was still there; he saw her curtains twitch and caught a flash of her white face. Across the road the gutted house stood as it had been, black, open to the air, abandoned. There was evidence that children had been there pulling the sticks and stones apart, scrawling slogans. A wind swirled up and blew a piece of grease-stained brown paper round Kevin's legs. It was reluctant to be dislodged. He kicked it away, with distaste. Relic of somebody's fish and chips. The litter was appalling, worse than it had been before, or perhaps it was that he noticed it more after the cleanness of the countryside. Old cigarette packets, sweet wrappers, cartons, greasy papers, broken glass, rusty tins. What a mess people made! Further along the pavement three small children were sitting on the ground playing, their hands and faces grimy with dirt. Bad dirt. Now if it were earth, wholesome brown soil! He was thankful that Brendan would not play here but would run across fields, climb stiles and trees, help with animals, breathe good fresh air.

Mr Paradise came out of the house. "Ah, Kevin, how are you, man? Coming up to see Mrs Paradise?" Later, said Kevin. They talked for a few minutes. Mr Paradise had work at the moment. He sounded chirpy. He walked off along the street whistling.

Kevin went the other way, passed the three children, saw that one was a Paradise. He took five pence from his pocket and gave it to them. They were on their feet in a flash and running for Mrs Hignett's shop.

At the end of the street Kevin paused. He felt a stranger here. The place was alien to him now; he could find nothing that meant anything to him. Maybe going back was no good; it was never the same. Kitty and Bill had never come back since they'd left. Bill said that he wouldn't have minded, he'd have liked a drink in the pub for old times' sake but Kitty refused, even though, at the time, she had not been unhappy living here. Kevin remembered Sadie's flushed face in Mrs Hignett's back shop. Sadie was glad to be back at any rate. She loved to talk, she loved the feeling of life hustling round her.

In the next street he came upon a group of kids, half-grown, smoking cigarette butts. The fingers that held the stubs lay close against their faces.

"You'll burn your mouths," he said.

"Drop dead!"

"Aren't you a Paradise?"

The boy's eyes rolled uninterestedly, not recognising Kevin. He went on puffing on his fiery butt.

"Got any fags, mister?" A boy got to his feet, sidled close. He came level with Kevin's shoulder.

"I don't smoke."

"Ach, come on, don't give us that: give us a fag." The boy tugged at Kevin's jacket.

"Sorry."

The other boys got up, surrounding him. There were five of them. One caught his boot against Kevin's ankle making him wince and the rest of the boys laugh.

"What about a bit of scratch then, eh, if you've no fags?"

"You've got the wrong man," said Kevin. He let his eyes travel round the group, amazed by the aggression in their faces. They were prepared to take him on, for the sake of a few cigarettes! "O.K., then, lads, I could be doing with a bit of elbow room."

"He could be doing with a bit of elbow room!"

"We like standing near you, mister."

"Well I don't like standing near you." Kevin pushed the boy back with the flat of his hand. He felt no anger, was quite cool. The boy half lost his balance, recovered and came for Kevin lunging out wildly. Then the others were upon him. He felt their boots flaying his shins.

It seemed crazy to have to fight a bunch of kids at his age but he had no choice: he could not stand like a dummy and let them beat him up. He was tall, broad and very strong from years of hard work and he knew too about boys fighting. He knocked two down easily, and the rest fled. He straightened his jacket, smoothed his hair. His shins and ankles throbbed.

"Come on," he said to the Paradise boy who crouched on the pavement nursing his hand. "I'm taking you home."

The boy did not speak. Kevin tried to talk to him, to tell him that life lived like that was pointless, he knew it himself, but he did not know if a word went home. Perhaps. He would rather have said it than not anyway. He would certainly tell such things to Brendan, but Mr Paradise had seven children and a struggle to survive, and he didn't blame the man if he didn't spend much time talking to his children. Blame was something that got more difficult to dish out, Kevin found, the older he got.

There was great excitement in the Paradise household. Gerald was sitting in a corner looking sheepish, saying little. But Maria was radiant and laughing.

"Kevin, look!" she cried, holding out a shiny, gleaming, honey-coloured guitar, brand new.

Kevin looked at Gerald. So that was what he had been saving for!

"Isn't it wonderful?" said Maria. She looked now as if she might cry instead of laugh.

"It's a beauty right enough," said Kevin, taking it between his hands to examine it.

"Gerald bought it for me."

"Play it, Maria." Kevin handed it back to her.

She sat down and began to pluck the strings, tuning them. The children quietened, squatted on the floor with their eyes turned expectantly on their sister.

"It was real kind of Gerald to buy it for Maria," said Mrs Paradise. "Real kind."

"She must keep it for herself," said Gerald, coming suddenly to life.

"Course she will. I'll see not another person put a finger on it," promised Maria's mother.

"You must not sell it," insisted Gerald.

"Sell it?" said Mrs Paradise. "Why would I do a thing like that?"

They all knew perfectly well why, and Gerald said again, "It belongs to Maria. I want her to keep it for herself."

"I'm sure Maria will see that she does," said Kevin.

Maria played and sang and smiled. Her audience clapped, cheered, called for more.

"They'll hear us all down the street," said Mrs Paradise happily.

"Anybody in?"

Sadie had arrived with Brendan. The baby was fussed over and admired and consented to go at once to Mrs Paradise.

"He likes my fat lap, don't you then, eh?" she said, bouncing him up and down on her knee.

"What's happened to your wrist, Kevin?" Sadie leaned over to look at a graze on Kevin's wrist. It was bleeding a little.

"Nothing much. I slipped and fell." He wrapped a handkerchief round it.

They spent most of the day at the Paradises'. And in the evening Mrs Hignett had a little party for them.

"You'll stay the night of course," she said. "I can squash you all in if you don't mind sleeping on the bed-settee. And Mrs Fiske says Gerald can put up on her couch."

Kevin had arranged for the boy to do the first milking on Sunday but they would have to leave early in the morning, he said, as he must get back to the farm as soon as possible.

"You and your cows!" said Sadie.

"You can't put them aside like you do a drill at the end of a day's work."

"Oh I know that well enough. Too well!"

Sadie was in an exuberant mood at Mrs Hignett's party, singing, dancing, laughing. Kevin was quieter; he sat in a corner, watching her, wondering. Perhaps this was her place, in the city, amongst people. But his was not; he knew that clearly. He had once been all for the city but too much had happened to turn him against it: violence and poverty for him were synonymous with it. He had never felt so well, so contented, as he was now on the farm. It was as though he had been looking for something, without knowing what, and he had found it.

"It's been a great day," said Sadie, as they settled down on Mrs Hignett's settee for the night. She was wide awake, in a chatty mood, wanting to talk over everything and everybody. She lay with her arms behind her head. "Gerald seems real keen on Maria. Do you think anything serious'll come of it?"

"I think they're just friendly-like. Nothing more. Anyway, they're too young." Kevin tried to find a place to put his hip, but failed.

"No younger than we were."

"We were daft."

"Huh!" snorted Sadie. "Speak for yourself."

"Things being what they were over there we got kind of forced into it."

Sadie sat up straight. "What d'you mean—forced into it?"

"Keep your hair on. I don't mean I didn't want to marry you, you know I did, but if we'd been left in peace we'd likely have taken longer, saved a bit first."

"So that we could have put a payment down on a nice semi like Kitty and Bill's?" She giggled suddenly. "Don't see us somehow."

"No, neither do I. Come on, love, give us a kiss and let's get to sleep. We don't want to sleep in in the morning."

"I know, the cows!"

Sadie went to sleep at once and slept soundly but Kevin passed a restless night, wakening intermittently to find himself hanging off the edge of the settee, and whenever he did drift off he dreamt. He dreamt that he was being mobbed by a huge crowd of menacing children, and all the faces of the children were the same: Brendan's. He awoke in a sweat. Light was filtering through the thin curtains. He got up, looked at Brendan in his carrycot, saw that his soft round face was peaceful and quite unlike what it had been in his nightmare. He lifted the curtain and looked out at the street. It was grey out there in the dawn light, and desolate. He missed the colour of the fields and trees, and the sight of the wide sky above them.

They dressed, had breakfast with Mrs Hignett who sat yawning in curlers and dressing gown saying it was a pity their visit had been so short, and then they said goodbye, promising to come back soon, extracting promises of visits to them.

"Now you will come this time won't you, Mrs Hignett?" demanded Sadie. "It's not far you know. Only about fifty miles."

Mrs Hignett crossed her nylon-quilted heart and swore she'd be out there before the month was up. Nothing would keep her from coming to see their house and Sadie's garden and Kevin's cows.

"Have you ever seen a cow close up?" said Sadie.

Mrs Hignett thought. "Can't say I have off-hand."

They left laughing. They travelled home, Sadie, Kevin, baby and dog, together. Gerald was staying for the day and would come in the evening.

"Lucky thing," said Sadie. "Could have done with a bit longer myself."

She spoke very little on the train to Chester, stared out of the window. Once on the bus she relaxed a little, played with Brendan on her lap and talked to him and Tamsin who would not keep still or quiet.

"We're like a travelling circus," said Kevin.

"I've always fancied circuses," said Sadie.

The bus stopped in the village.

"Look, there's Mrs Hughes!" Sadie waved, held Tamsin up against the window, waggled her paw too. Tamsin barked and stood on Brendan's face. Brendan cried.

The bus started off again, turned down the road running along beside the Ellersley estate. Kevin's eyes quickened. Boys, but the place looked trim and good! It must be a fine thing to have a bit of land of your own, even a small bit, cultivate it and tend it and graze your own beasts. Who knows but one of these days ...?

"Hey, wake up!" Sadie was digging him in the ribs. "It's our stop."

They got off the bus, let it pass and then they turned to open their own gate.

"Look, Kev, there's a new tulip open." Sadie ran forward and went down on her knees in the grass. "What a gorgeous orangey-pink! Isn't it lovely?"

" 'Deed it is. It's a beauty all right." Kevin set down the carrycot and stretched himself wide. "Think I'll cut the grass today. It could be doing with it."

Tamsin was released from the lead which she so much disliked and galloped happily about the garden investigating every nook and cranny. Her red-gold tail wagged enthusiastically.

"She's glad to be back," said Sadie.

"Are you?"

She nodded.

"Honestly?"

"Yes, honestly. Oh I know I miss all those friends. I wish they were nearer. But they're not. And I'd rather be here with the garden and the flowers and Tamsin running round. Did you see how dirty the streets were? And I was beginning to cough, the air's so bad. I'd have had the Mersey throat before I was done if we'd stayed. I couldn't live in it again, Kevin, not after this."

"I'm real glad to hear you saying that, Sadie." Kevin felt as if a stone had rolled off his heart. For a moment during his depression of the night he had wondered if Sadie might ask him to bring her back to the city. "What about a bit of lunch then eh? I'm starving. Come on and I'll give you a hand."

Gerald came home on the last bus. Sadie made cocoa and they sat round the fire to drink it. The day had cooled after tea and Kevin had set the logs in the grate alight.

Sadie sighed with pleasure. "We were just saying the day, Gerald, that we'd be happy enough to stay here for ever. What about you?"

He shrugged, drank his cocoa.

"You like it don't you?"

"Yes."

"Well then?"

"There's no need for anyone to think what they're going to do for ever, Sadie," said Kevin.

"Matter of fact," said Gerald abruptly, "I'm leaving at the end of summer. When the racing season's over."

"What for?" cried Sadie.

"I'm going back to Ireland. I've been making inquiries. There's a stable in Wexford that I think'll have me. Sure Ireland's a great country for horses. The best in the world. And it's my country too."

It's my country too. The words fell amongst them, quietening them.

"Think I'll be off to my bed. I've a heavy day on tomorrow." Gerald got up, stood awkwardly for a moment. "I'm sorry. I'm right grateful to the two of you ..."

"We know that," said Kevin. "You have to do what you think's best, Gerald."

"And you know you'll always be welcome here," said Sadie.

After Gerald had gone to bed, Sadie and Kevin sat by the smouldering logs soaking up the last bit of heat.

"D'you know, I'll miss him?" said Sadie. "I never thought

I'd say that! Oh he's not the easiest of mortals to get on with, he can be difficult at times, moody as anything, but he's not a bad lad. Not bad at all."

"We have to let him go, though."

"Oh yes. Of course."

"At least we gave him a chance when he needed it. But now he'll have to make his own way." Kevin lifted a strand of Sadie's hair and smoothed it back from her warm face. "Just as we've done."

007566970

Lingard   c.1
  A proper place.